"I don't need you there to hold my hand."

He held up both hands. "I wouldn't dream of it. Friend."

"Neighbor," she mumbled as she walked away.

Dane followed Lucy inside. He shouldn't have. He should have gotten back to work. Instead he walked behind her, ignoring the tense set of her shoulders and the fact that she didn't want him along for this journey.

"Stop thinking about me." She shot the comment over her shoulder as she walked through the kitchen. "I'm not a project. I don't need to be fixed. Go do whatever good deed you were going to do here today."

"I'm replacing light fixtures and repairing some sockets. You're not on my to-do list."

He couldn't stop himself, though. For the last few years he had focused all his energy on the ranch and his daughter.

The last thing he wanted was to get caught up in Lucy's messy life. But here he was, intrigued and unable to walk away.

Brenda Minton lives in the Ozarks with her husband, children, cats, dogs and strays. She is a pastor's wife, Sunday-school teacher, coffee addict and sleep deprived. Not in that order. Her dream to be an author for Harlequin started somewhere in the pages of a romance novel about a young American woman stranded in a Spanish castle. Her dream came true, and twenty-plus books later, she is an author hoping to inspire young girls to dream.

Books by Brenda Minton

Love Inspired

Bluebonnet Springs

Second Chance Rancher

Martin's Crossing

A Rancher for Christmas
The Rancher Takes a Bride
The Rancher's Second Chance
The Rancher's First Love
Her Rancher Bodyguard
Her Guardian Rancher

Lone Star Cowboy League: Boys Ranch

The Rancher's Texas Match

Lone Star Cowboy League

A Reunion for the Rancher

Visit the Author Profile page at Harlequin.com for more titles.

Second Chance Rancher

Brenda Minton

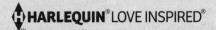

If you purchased this book without a cover you should be aware
that this book is stolen property. It was reported as "unsold and
destroyed" to the publisher, and neither the author nor the
publisher has received any payment for this "stripped book."

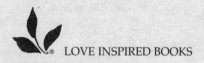

LOVE INSPIRED BOOKS

Recycling programs
for this product may
not exist in your area.

ISBN-13: 978-0-373-62291-7

Second Chance Rancher

Copyright © 2017 by Brenda Minton

All rights reserved. Except for use in any review, the reproduction
or utilization of this work in whole or in part in any form by any
electronic, mechanical or other means, now known or hereinafter
invented, including xerography, photocopying and recording, or in
any information storage or retrieval system, is forbidden without
the written permission of the editorial office, Love Inspired Books,
195 Broadway, New York, NY 10007 U.S.A.

This is a work of fiction. Names, characters, places and incidents are
either the product of the author's imagination or are used fictitiously, and
any resemblance to actual persons, living or dead, business establishments,
events or locales is entirely coincidental.

This edition published by arrangement with Love Inspired Books.

® and TM are trademarks of Love Inspired Books, used under license.
Trademarks indicated with ® are registered in the United States Patent
and Trademark Office, the Canadian Intellectual Property Office and in
other countries.

www.Harlequin.com

Printed in U.S.A.

For God has not given us a spirit of fear and
timidity, but of power, love and self discipline.
—*2 Timothy* 1:7

To my family for the love and encouragement
they've given me over the years.

To Melissa, for the opportunity to
continue writing the books I love.
And Giselle, for all her work in this process.
Thank you both for keeping me on track.

Chapter One

Late morning sun in his eyes, Dane Scott thought he couldn't be seeing right. There was an old Chevy truck tangled up in the fencerow and a half-dozen head of his cattle grazing in the ditch. He pulled to the side of the road and got out. His dog jumped off the back of the truck and followed him down the slope. As he drew closer, Dane prepared himself, hoping he wouldn't find anyone inside the truck that he knew belonged to his neighbors, the Palermos.

Fortunately the truck was empty. The tires were bogged down in mud, compliments of two days of rain and a driver who had tried to back out of the mess. Barbed wire from the fence was wrapped around the passenger side tires.

At least he could surmise that seventeen-year-old Maria Palermo wasn't injured. The big problem was, who to call. The Palermo family was what the good folks of Bluebonnet Spring, Texas, called "a mess." That was usually followed by a "bless their hearts" or "it wasn't really their fault."

The most functional member of the family was Lucy Palermo. But last he'd heard, she was a couple of hun-

dred miles south, near Austin. The twin brothers, Alex
and Marcus, were somewhere riding bulls. Their mother
was in California with husband number three.

Dane knew Maria was home alone and running wild.
Even when her brothers showed up and pretended to be
responsible, she was on her own.

He guessed he could call Essie Palermo, great-aunt
of the four siblings and owner of Essie's Diner in Bluebonnet Springs. Essie lamented the children of her late
nephew. She said a little religion wouldn't have hurt
them, but the kind they'd gotten from their own father
had wounded them to the core.

Dane pulled the keys out of the ignition of the abandoned truck and walked back up the embankment to
the road. He pulled his hat low and scanned the field
where another two hundred head of Black Angus cattle
grazed. Good thing they hadn't spotted the truck-sized
hole in the fence.

At the moment it didn't matter who he called. He
had to get that truck out of his field and patch up the
fence. As he headed for his vehicle, a dark blue truck
parked behind his. Even with a glare on the windshield,
he could see the driver, her dark hair pulled back and
a big frown tugging at her mouth.

Lucy Palermo. The oldest of the Palermo siblings,
and the last person he expected to see on this stretch of
the road. A year younger than his thirty years, she had
reasons for avoiding her childhood home. And they had
reasons for avoiding each other.

She was out of her truck and heading his way, cutting
short his trip down memory lane. Not that he wanted
to go there. He opened the toolbox on the back of his
truck and pulled out gloves and wire cutters. From the

frown on her face he could tell she was half mad and half worried.

"She's not in the truck so she must be okay." He guessed that might ease her worry, and then she could focus on being mad.

"She needs to be locked up," Lucy said on a huff, her gaze shooting to the wrecked truck.

He gave her a quick look, trying to come to terms with the woman at his side, because the girl he'd known hadn't been this cool person with the clipped tone. A smile took him by surprise but he tamped it down because he didn't need her ire. That's exactly what he would get if she knew he'd even dared to think of that girl and that summer. It was safer to keep the conversation on Maria, her little sister.

"She's just a kid."

She responded with rapid-fire Portuguese, then briefly closed her eyes and shook her head.

"She's a kid who ran her truck through a neighbor's fence and left." She spoke again in English.

He shook his head and walked away, because she knew better. Lucy followed, still talking. He hid a smile as she continued to rant about their mother leaving town, her irresponsible brothers and the call from Aunt Essie telling her she was needed in Bluebonnet Springs.

"She didn't know what to do." He defended her aunt.

"I know. And it isn't her responsibility. I should have been here."

He stopped because something needed to be said. She nearly ran into him, so with his free hand he reached out to steady her. Her dark eyes snapped as she looked down at his hand on her arm, not saying a word, but clearly reinforcing the Don't Touch policy.

Yeah, that was the Lucy he remembered. She'd been wearing that Hands Off sign for a long time. "You're here now," he offered. "Maybe if you stay, you can help her out."

Wrong words. Her dark eyes narrowed. Try as he might, he was a man and he noticed that even spitting mad, she was beautiful. Not the flowery, glossy kind of beauty, but strong and wildly feminine even in jeans, a plain T-shirt and boots.

She scrubbed a hand over her face and sighed. "I plan on staying. And I'm sorry about the fence. I'll help you get your cattle back in, and then I'll see to getting the fence fixed."

They stood side by side studying the wrecked truck and the fence. Dane's dog, Pete, a black-and-white border collie, sniffed the tires.

"I'm sure she'll be okay, Lucy. She's been through a lot."

"I know she's been through a lot." She kept a steady gaze on the truck but he saw moisture gather in her eyes. "I thought Maria was staying with Aunt Essie."

"I think she might have stayed there for a few weeks but eventually she moved back to the ranch."

"I can't say that I blame her. Essie is used to living alone. But I wish someone had told me our mother had skipped town again. If nothing else, I could have taken Maria to Austin with me."

Dane shot her a look, knowing she was talking more to herself than to him. She confirmed that by giving him a hard stare that seemed to ask what he was looking at. So he shrugged it off and started clipping wires wrapped around the wheels of the truck.

He wasn't getting involved. He was just going to fix

his fence and head home to his own life. Lucy Palermo could take care of her problems. He'd take care of his.

After pushing the truck out of the way, Lucy had helped Dane get his cattle back. They'd patched the fence but she promised she'd be back to make it right. As she headed up the dirt drive that led to the home she'd been raised in, she felt that old familiar tightening around her heart. She recognized it as panic. A few deep breaths helped to ease the pain. There was nothing here to fear. Her father was gone. His life claimed by a bull he'd hoped would be his ticket to the big time.

Her mother wasn't in the kitchen pretending there was nothing wrong with a man who randomly drank, quoted the Bible and then beat his children for the slightest infraction.

Lucy parked in the circle drive, just a dozen feet from the front steps of the house. It no longer looked like a home, not with the lawn covered in weeds, flowers growing wild up the posts that supported the porch roof and no lights glimmering from inside. The one thing that had been a constant had been the facade of this home. It had looked like a house where a happy family lived. The house had been a real metaphor for their lives. Picturesque on the outside, dark and painful on the inside.

As she headed for the front door she gave herself a pep talk. She didn't have to stay here. She could take Maria with her back to Austin. Why should either of them stay in Bluebonnet now that Maria would be graduating high school? It seemed like the perfect solution.

She stepped through the front door, chastising herself for reliving the past. The house was quiet except for the ticking of the grandfather clock in the dining room. The air conditioner hadn't been turned on and the temperature inside must have been at least ninety degrees. It felt cooler outside than in. To top it off, the place had the distinct smell of neglect. The trash hadn't been taken out. The dog had been left to run inside. Her mother had abandoned her duties. Again.

That left Lucy to pick up the pieces and keep her siblings on track. At twenty-nine she was tired of being the family glue, but since there was no one else, she would do what needed to be done.

She would clean up the mess. She would find her younger sister. She would make sure her twin brothers were clean and sober. For years, since their father's death, the family was like a spring that had been coiled up tight and then turned loose. They'd all gone off in different directions, a little wild, a lot unpredictable.

She'd picked the Army, even before her father's death, because it had seemed like the antithesis to her childhood. Every day in the military she'd known the time to get up, to eat and to go to bed. She'd usually known what each day would require. Most importantly, it had meant being thousands of miles from Bluebonnet.

There had been surprises. There had been pain. And death. But she'd survived. The same way she'd survived her childhood.

"Maria, where are you?" Lucy yelled. From the back of the ranch house, the dog barked. Maria didn't respond, but Lucy guessed if she followed the bark, she'd find her sister.

She opened the door at the end of the hall. Maria was passed out on her bed. The dog growled from the pillow next to her. Lucy scanned the disaster of a bedroom. Clothes covered nearly every surface. The chair by the window, the dresser, the floor. It looked like a department store had exploded. The windows were wide-open, letting in the heat of late May.

What a mess.

"Stupid poodle." Maria, dark hair tangled and smudges beneath her eyes, reached in a half slumber and pushed the dog off the bed.

"Be nice to the dog," Lucy warned.

Maria sat up quickly, then held her head and groaned. "Go away."

"Right, because a seventeen-year-old can be trusted to take care of herself."

"Marcus and Alex are here. They're adults. And I'm almost eighteen."

"Our brothers are in Waco and we both know that. I got a call from Essie, letting me know you were running wild and she's taking care of the livestock. But you, on the other hand…"

"She should mind her own business." Maria fell back on the pillow and covered her head with a blanket. "I hate you."

"Right, because alcohol is your friend and I'm not. How long has our mother been gone? And why aren't you with her?"

"She went to California a couple of months ago. She and husband number three are back in love. I don't like to be a third wheel. And I haven't been drinking."

"Of course you haven't. Get up out of that bed. You have a fence to fix."

"What?" She brushed a hand through the tangles of her curly, chestnut hair.

"You ran through Dane Scott's fence, Maria. Last night. You even left the truck where you wrecked it." Lucy shook her head and gave her sister another long look. "Get up. I'll help with the fence but I'm not doing all the work."

"Poor Lucy, she has to do everything. And I wasn't drinking." The blanket she'd held to her chin dropped, revealing a rounded tummy. Lucy closed her eyes, hoping what she'd seen wasn't real, wasn't happening.

"You're pregnant." She said it softly, waiting for Maria to deny it.

"Yeah. Surprise! And I wasn't drinking. A deer ran in front of my truck."

"No one told me." Lucy had been busy working in Austin as a bodyguard. She'd had her own life, happily far from the family drama, even though she occasionally got calls to come home and fix things. But now the drama had landed in her lap.

"No. We didn't tell you. Last time you were home I wasn't showing."

"Everyone knows? Even Mom?"

"She doesn't know. She isn't observant. Essie told me it was my place to tell you."

"How far along?"

Maria looked young. And lost. She was having a baby. "Close to five months," she answered in a quiet voice.

"Okay, well, we'll figure this out." With that, Lucy left the room, the hungry poodle fast on her heels.

A truck pulled up as she washed dishes. Dane had towed the old farm truck back to the house for her. She let out a long sigh, rinsed the plate she had just washed and walked to the front door. Dane Scott stood in the yard, eyeing the mess that had once been the Palermo ranch. A frown settled on his too-handsome, too-tan, too-everything face. He pushed back the cowboy hat that shaded his features and pulled the sunglasses off his too-straight nose.

Lucy wanted to go back inside, lock the door and pretend she'd never been sixteen and in love with Dane. Heat climbed into her cheeks thinking about her teen self and how she'd dreamed he'd take her away from this ranch and her father.

That was all ancient history, years of water under the proverbial bridge.

"Don't just stand there drooling," Maria whispered from behind her, humor lacing her tone. "Put him in his place. Never let them see you dream, sis."

Lucy walked down the steps, pretending Maria hadn't spoken.

"Dane." She grabbed the yapping poodle as it ran circles around his stock dog. Other people had real cattle dogs. The Palermo family had a poodle that couldn't find the door to go outside and wouldn't know a cow from a tree. "Thank you for towing it home for me. Maria and I will fix the fence."

His blue eyes narrowed, then his gaze shifted to the point beyond her left shoulder where she knew Maria must be standing. He nodded just slightly as he refocused on her.

"You don't have to fix it, Lucy. I'll send a couple of my men over to finish up the repairs."

"We're responsible. We'll fix it." She kept her tone even, because she wouldn't argue the point.

He tipped his hat back and leveled those blue eyes of his on her. "I'll fix the fence. While I'm here I wanted to make sure I can renew my lease for the three hundred acres."

"Of course you can. Why wouldn't we keep the

agreement?" She wondered if there was something she didn't know. Something she should know.

He shrugged. "I guess I thought you were going to stick around and might want to use that land."

She glanced back at her obviously pregnant sister. The teenager was sitting on one of the older rocking chairs on the covered front porch that ran the length of the house.

"I guess I won't be going anywhere, not for a while. But I'm not going to need that land. I'll make do with the two hundred we've been using."

"You didn't know?" Dane's voice was smooth, quiet and concerned.

He meant about Maria. She briefly closed her eyes and shook her head. In that moment it would have been easy to return to the girl she'd been, the one who had confided in him, shared secrets with him.

No, she told herself. That was a long time ago. A dozen years might as well have been a lifetime because they'd both gone through things. They'd changed. The kids they'd been, those two teens who had met up while riding horses, or in town every once in a while, those two were long gone.

"No. I didn't know," she answered. She wasn't getting the Sister of the Year award. "It looks as if I should have come home sooner. I tried a few times, but work…"

She didn't owe him explanations. He was a neighbor. He leased part of their land. He wasn't their keeper.

He was her past. A very unhappy part of her past.

"Understandable," he answered, anyway. The one word was meant to let her off the hook. She didn't need that, either.

"No, it isn't. But I'm here now. And it looks as if I have a lot of work to do. Starting with your fence." She let her gaze slide away from his piercing eyes to a stable that needed repairs, a wood fence that had fallen down in places and a lawn that was overgrown.

In the distance an ATV could be heard. She glanced west, the direction the sound came from.

"That would be Essie, coming to give me her opinion of the place and my life," Lucy said, more to herself than to her neighbor.

"She does have opinions." He grinned as he said it. They all knew Essie. She ran a café in town and had her own small spread about a mile down the road.

In the midst of the worst of her nephew's religious antics, Essie had rebelled. She'd refused to attend his services, her first offense. And then she'd tried to stop him from beating Lucy. That had earned her a black eye and an escort from the premises. It wasn't until after his death that Essie was allowed back on the property.

"Yes, she does have opinions." Lucy watched the four-wheeler and the woman controlling it, a bright red helmet covering her now-graying hair.

"I'll unhitch your truck and leave it by the garage. But let me know if you need anything. And don't worry about the fence. I can get it taken care of." He gave them a parting nod with a tilt of his white cowboy hat before he climbed back in his big Ford King Ranch and drove slowly in the direction of the garage, their old truck clunking along behind him.

"The temperature goes up ten degrees every time he's near. Hot. Hot. Hot." Maria appeared at Lucy's side, a cheeky grin on her face. She took the poodle from Lucy. "I'll get changed and we can get to work on this place. But you might want to go splash some cold water on your face first."

Lucy shook her head and walked away from her little sister, who was grinning as if this was all a big joke and they weren't in serious trouble.

Chapter Two

Lucy headed for the barn where Essie had parked. Essie shot her a critical look, shaking her head as she hooked her helmet on the handlebars of the ATV. Her long gray hair was pulled back in a ponytail. Twin slashes of rose-tinted blush dotted her cheeks. She was dressed in jeans and a T-shirt with a photo of downtown Bluebonnet Springs on the front.

"What's Dane Scott doing here?" Essie said with the faintest trace of an accent. She'd moved to the United States forty years ago. Her husband, Emit Jackson, had been an American soldier. She'd loved him at first sight and would have followed him anywhere, she'd always told them.

Lucy's father, Jesse Palermo, had arrived in Texas ten years later. He'd moved to the States when his bull riding career had been at its peak and the big money had been found outside his native Brazil.

It should have been obvious why Dane was there, but Lucy could play along. "He towed the truck home."

Her aunt gave her a half grin. "He's still a good-looking man."

"I suppose, but he's a bit young for you."

Essie cackled at that. "Pity, but it's true. But then, I was never in love with him."

Had she been in love? It had been years ago and she'd convinced herself that it had simply been infatuation. Or maybe she'd been attracted to him because he'd seemed strong and safe.

She no longer needed a man to make her feel safe. She no longer needed to escape this life.

"I guess you saw your sister?" Essie asked as she sat on the edge of the ATV seat.

"Yes, I saw her." Lucy didn't know what else to say to her aunt. Her sister was pregnant. As the old saying went, "the cow was already out of the barn."

Essie gave Lucy a long look with dark eyes that made a person squirm. "I hope you weren't too hard on her."

"I wasn't." Lucy sighed. "To be honest, I'm not sure what to do."

"Aren't you?" Essie's mouth pulled down. "I'm not going to tell you that she's your responsibility, Lucy. But she has to be someone's responsibility. She's not even eighteen and she doesn't have anyone. Your mother doesn't have a maternal bone in her body. Your brothers are chasing pipe dreams. It's like that poor girl is collateral damage. I love her but she doesn't want to live with an old woman. And I sure don't speak teen girl."

"It's a different language," Lucy admitted. "I don't know that I've ever spoken it."

Essie's eyes softened. "I know and I'm sorry. You were all victims and I wish I could have done more for you."

Lucy nodded, her gaze again drifting across the

property. It was easier to deal with the land, the house and not her emotional well-being. "It's a mess."

"Yes, it is." Essie followed the direction of Lucy's gaze.

They were both talking about more than the condition of the ranch.

"I'm not sure what to do about Maria." Lucy leaned against the fence and watched as the few head of cattle stopped to graze before moving on to the water trough.

"Not much you can do. I don't think she wants to marry the boy." Essie got off the ATV and joined Lucy as she crossed to the fence to look out at the property. "I worry that she won't go to college. She's a smart girl and I don't want her to give up on her dreams."

Her sister had dreams. Lucy tried to remember what that had been like, to dream of something other than making it through a night without nightmares.

"Take time and get to know her, Lucy," Essie said. "She's someone you will probably like."

Lucy nodded, her gaze remaining on the cattle. "I'll talk to her. I'm not sure what I'm supposed to say."

"Talking is a start. She would probably like to have someone around. She gets lonely out here. When a kid get lonely, they get in trouble."

Lucy thought about her own teen years. She'd been lonely and she'd also found trouble.

Essie patted her arm and headed for her four-wheeler. "I have to get to the café. I hired that silly Bea Maxwell to cook when I'm not there but I worry about leaving her alone. Why don't you girls get cleaned up and come in for lunch? My treat."

"I'm not sure. It looks like I have a fence to rebuild and a few things around here that can't be put off."

"Supper, then?"

Lucy nodded in agreement and watched as her aunt slid the helmet over her head. Essie smiled at her and then, quickly, before Lucy could react, stepped forward and embraced her. Lucy stiffened beneath the unaccustomed gesture but Essie didn't let go. She hugged a little tighter and finished the embrace by patting her on the back.

"It will all work out, *chica*. Trust God that He has a plan."

Lucy stepped back, putting some distance between them, and drew in a deep breath, telling herself she hadn't needed or wanted that hug. "I think I'll leave the faith to you, Aunt Essie. I'll deal with the ranch and making sure Maria is healthy. You and God work out the rest."

Essie laughed a little. "Oh, don't you worry. Me and God are on very good terms."

"I know."

Unfortunately Lucy and God were another matter altogether. She'd had a childhood of God, sermons, the Bible and beatings. She avoided church and people who wanted to help her "get right with the Lord." She admired people with genuine faith. She knew that it mattered. But she couldn't make the walls disappear. The fortress around her heart was strong, built one beating at a time.

She headed for the house. Again the putrid smell of neglect hit her the moment she walked through the door. First things first—she needed some bleach and pine cleaner. Maria was in the kitchen scavenging in the fridge. She mumbled something about "nothing to eat" and that she was eating for two. "Don't people realize the tadpole needs nourishment?"

Lucy couldn't help but smile. The mischievous little

girl Lucy had known had survived, still smart-mouthed and funny. She was the one good thing to come out of this place. And she could still smile. Lucy envied her sister.

"Essie said she'd feed us tonight. Until then, is there anything in the cabinets that isn't spoiled?" Lucy grabbed a bottle of water out of the door of the fridge, and then gagged a little. "What's in there?"

Maria slammed the door of the fridge, put a hand to her mouth and ran.

Lucy followed her sister to the bathroom door.

"Don't come in," Maria grumbled.

"I'm not, but I'm here if you need me." She leaned against the wall and waited.

Her little sister was having a baby. It would take time to wrap her mind around this new reality. Maria had been seven when Lucy left home to join the Army. She'd been a terror in pigtails, with a dirty face and into all kinds of trouble.

A bittersweet memory surfaced. Maria, insecure, crawling in bed with Lucy after everyone else went to sleep.

Now that little girl was going to be a mother.

"Luce?"

"I'm here."

"I don't want a baby," Maria sobbed.

Lucy took that as an invitation to step into the bathroom. Maria was sitting on the edge of the bathtub, her eyes closed, perspiration dampening her brow. She was pale and thin. No, not thin. The baby bump beneath her T-shirt was obvious.

Lucy shoved back the dozens of responses to her sister's statement. It wouldn't do any good to tell Maria she should have thought about wanting a baby before she'd gotten herself pregnant. She couldn't change what had happened. Instead there were obvious consequences. A child. A baby with two kids as parents, kids who didn't want to be parents.

"No, I'm sure you don't want a baby." Lucy didn't know what else to say. Maria scrunched her nose and frowned. "Sorry, Maria. I'm not sure what to say. But I'm here. We'll get through this."

"You've been telling me that for a long time," Maria whispered, looking young and frightened in this new role life had cast her in.

But not by herself.

Lucy sighed and remembered back, to nights when she'd tried to reassure her little sister.

Long-ago nights when Maria would crowd onto the twin bed in the room the two shared. They would hug each other and Lucy would whisper that it would be okay. Tiny Maria would pat her cheek or trace the bruise on Lucy's face.

She'd never thought about it before, but the two of them had survived the way soldiers survive—together.

"I guess I've never known what else to say, Maria. We will get through this. Yes, you'll have a baby. But it isn't the end of the world."

"It is for me."

Lucy sank down to sit next to her sister. "It isn't. I promise. You'll graduate soon. You can take classes online."

Maria gasped and looked at her. "I graduated early. In December. You didn't know. I wondered, because you weren't here."

Stunned, they sat in silence for several minutes. "I'm sorry I wasn't here."

"We didn't make a big deal out of it. I got my diploma. Mom told me I'm brilliant. Alex sent me a post-card from California, and Marcus called."

And Lucy had done nothing.

Maria patted her leg, a reassuring gesture for a young sister to give an older sibling. "Don't let it bother you. Mom is like that. She probably thought you were too busy. Or that you wouldn't want to be here."

"I should have been here. I wish you'd called me."

Maria leaned against her. "I want to be a doctor."

Another thing she hadn't known about her little sister.

"That's pretty impressive."

"I'm going to give the baby up for adoption."

The words hung between them for several minutes. Maria remained quiet, her eyes closed, her breathing ragged. Lucy took a minute to process what her sister had told her because it felt as if she were trying to avoid land mines as she navigated the situation she'd walked into. When Aunt Essie had called and told her to come home, she hadn't given the slightest bit of a hint to what Lucy was walking into. Lucy had convinced herself she was heading home to take care of livestock and nothing more.

"What about the father?" she asked belatedly.

Maria shrugged. "He told me he isn't ready to be a dad. And I know he isn't. Besides, he left last month. He joined the Army."

"Whatever you decide about the baby, I'm here for you." It was the only response that made any sense. Of course she would be there for her sister.

But she hadn't been, had she? Guilt coiled around her heart, giving it a tight squeeze.

"Are you going to leave again?" Maria didn't move;

her head remained on Lucy's shoulder. "I'm tired of being alone."

"I'm not going anywhere." She glanced at her watch. "I take that back. I'm going to town. We need real food in this house and cleaning supplies."

"Dane's fence?" Maria reminded.

"I'll take care of the fence."

She had a list of things to take care of. Her sister, for now, was at the top of that list. She also needed to call Daron McKay and Boone Wilder, her partners in the bodyguard business and let them know she wouldn't be back, not for a while. Maybe not ever.

That was the last thing she wanted to consider at this moment, that she might have to give up her career.

Maria gave her a quirky grin. "Dane Scott is yummy, thirty and single. If I was you, I'd take my time mending that fence."

The only fence she and Dane Scott would be mending was the one Maria had driven the truck through. And when it was finished, he could stay on his side and she'd stay on hers. He was nothing more than a distraction and she didn't like to be distracted.

Dane followed the Realtor, Jeff Owens, across the lawn. They'd driven most of the property, toured the barns, the stable and the house. The only thing left to do was sign on the dotted line. But when a man was signing a piece of paper that would effectively put not just a property but a family tradition up for sale, signing wasn't an easy thing to do. He was a rancher. His parents, grandparents and great-grandparents had been ranchers.

Being a father, a good one, meant making sacrifices.

Haven, his sister, younger by three years, joined them. She studied him as he looked the paper over.

"You're sure?" she asked as they leaned against Jeff Owens's truck. The man was discreet. That was the reason for choosing him.

"If you are," Dane answered. "It's a family decision. You know that Mom and Dad are settled in Dallas. They have no intention of coming back. So that leaves it up to the two of us."

"I know." She shifted away, scanning the horizon, the land that belonged to them. "I know you have solid reasons for doing this. I know that I'm not here a lot. It just seems like we're walking away from what our grandparents built."

"I know." He'd had the same thought too many times to count. That was why he hadn't yet put his signature on the paper in front of him. "If it wasn't for Issy..."

His daughter meant everything to him.

Haven touched his arm and gave a quick shake of her head. "Don't ever apologize for doing what's best for her."

"Is it best?"

Jeff cleared his throat. "What about a three-month listing?"

Haven shrugged.

Dane glanced from his sister to the paper. A three month contract would give them the opportunity to sell. And the opportunity to make sure this was what they wanted.

"I think that would work. No signs. No listing it publicly. I don't want our neighbors to know that the place is up for sale."

"Discreet is my middle name. If I have buyers looking for a property that fits this description, I'll call you."

Jeff pulled a briefcase out of his truck. "I have the paperwork we wrote up last week. I just need your signature."

Dane accepted a pen and the contract, and after a deep breath and a prayer, he signed. Then Haven signed. It was done. Jeff shook their hands and left.

"I have to go. Issy and Lois are reading a book." Haven glanced at her watch. "Lois is a gem."

"I couldn't do it without her," Dane acknowledged. He started to walk away. "She's going to be gone, what with her daughter having a baby. But Maria Palermo said she'd help out."

"Maria is really good with her, Dane. Let her help."

Let someone else into his daughter's life. Yes, he knew that he needed to ease up a little. He had to trust people. He had to trust Issy. It was easy to say, but then he would remember how it had felt to hold his little girl at night while she cried for her mama. A mother who had walked away without a backward glance.

"Was that Lucy Palermo I saw sliding back into town?" Haven asked. He could hear the humor in her tone. Great that she thought it was amusing.

When a man put a woman at risk, he had a hard time recovering his sense of humor. He'd been too young to realize that their secret meetings would create such an uproar at the Palermo ranch. He hadn't known how to handle it when she'd told him they were done, that she couldn't see him anymore. After that she'd closed herself off from him and everyone else.

"Yeah, it was Lucy."

"I'm sorry. I shouldn't have brought it up."

He shrugged and managed a smile for his sister. "It's okay. She's here to take charge of Maria and the ranch."

"She won't stay long. She never does."

No, she didn't. He didn't blame her.

"I've got to head to town and pick up some supplies I ordered from the feed store. Need anything?"

"No, nothing." Haven glanced at her watch. "Pastor Matthews called. He's putting together the groups that will help with the shelter renovation."

"I'll call him. Or stop by there. Tell Lois I won't be gone long."

The shelter. As he got in his truck he wondered if anyone had told Lucy what the new pastor had done with her father's church.

Less than a half mile from his driveway he saw Lucy's truck parked on the side of the road. She was in the ditch, pulling fence. She stopped, wiped her face with the bandanna tied around her neck and went back to work. She had to know he was there but she didn't spare him a glance. He smiled. She'd always been so self-contained.

Except that summer thirteen years ago. It had all started when he saw her riding the back fence of the Palermo property. She was pretending to check fence but later she told him she'd just needed to get away from her dad so she'd offered to clean out the weeds along that fence. They'd been neighbors their whole lives but that summer something shifted. When he saw her on that horse, he saw a woman, not the little girl in raggedy clothes and pigtails he'd always known.

But she hadn't been a woman. They'd both been kids. They hadn't been mature enough to handle what they felt, or her home life.

He got out of his truck and joined her at the fence, pulling on gloves before grabbing the line of barbed wire she was stringing between new posts. She gave him a quick look but kept working.

"I told you I'd have a couple of my guys do this," he said as they worked together.

"I told you I would do it myself."

"Stubborn," he said with a smile and some admiration.

"Yeah, you've said that before. So let's not go back there."

"Because you still won't talk about it?" Suddenly he wished he'd taken her advice and let it go. There was no point in going back.

Lucy stopped working. She pulled off her gloves and shoved them in her pockets. "You were right. Let your guys fix this. I'll cover the cost."

She stomped away. He let her get a few feet ahead of him, then he followed. He didn't really know when to quit. It was something his mom had been telling him for as long as he could remember.

"Lucy, wait." He caught up with her on the shoulder of the road. "I'm sorry for pushing."

"Good, so don't do it again. I'm here to take care of my sister and to make things right on our ranch. I don't have time for anything else. I don't *want* anything else."

That couldn't be any clearer than the nose on his face. It was the same message she'd given him that long-ago summer.

"I understand." He held out a gloved hand. She gave it a long look before accepting the gesture. "Friends?"

"Neighbors." But she smiled as she said it.

Neighbors? He could handle that.

"How's the bodyguard business?" he asked as they headed for their vehicles.

"Busy." She folded her arms in front of herself. "Is this really what we're going to do?"

"Safe conversation. Isn't that what you want?" He

should walk away. Because nothing felt safe with Lucy.
But he kept going.

"Let's stick to the weather."

"Okay." He glanced up at the blue sky. "I sure love
spring but we need rain."

She walked away from him but he saw a flash of a
smile on her face. "I have to go."

He debated telling her about the shelter—he didn't
want her to be blindsided. If she didn't know about the
church, she should.

"Lucy, they have a new pastor at the church. They've
changed the name."

She froze, her hand on the truck door. "Okay. Good
to know."

"It isn't the same." They both knew what that meant.
Her dad had called it a church but it had been a cult.
He'd controlled his flock, taken their money and left
them empty and lost.

He'd done the most damage to his own family.

"I'm sure it's not," she answered.

"It's a good place now. They're starting a shelter for
abused women."

Women like the ones who had attended the church
her father pastored. A church where men were encouraged to force their wives and children into submission.

"I'm glad to hear that," she said with a catch in her
voice.

He started to reach for her but he knew she wouldn't
welcome his touch. The very last thing he needed to be
doing was building a connection. She was still broken.
He had his own life now. He had a daughter who needed
his full attention and he didn't have time for relationships that were destined not to end well.

"You should stop by and see what they're doing,"

he suggested. "It might be good for you, to see it in a new light."

"I'll think about it. But you don't know me well enough to give me advice."

"I'm trying to be a friend," he offered. "Sorry, a neighbor."

She smiled, the gesture softening her features in a way he hadn't expected. "Neighbors bring casseroles but they don't pry."

"This neighbor isn't much of a cook," he confessed.

"Really, Dane, thank you for telling me about the church. I've had enough surprises for one day."

"You're welcome."

She glanced at her watch. "I have to get ready for dinner. Essie wants us to eat with her tonight."

As he watched her drive away, he realized what Essie had done. Lucy was in for another surprise. One she probably wasn't going to like.

Chapter Three

Main Street Bluebonnet was busy for early evening. It took Lucy by surprise when she cruised down the two-block-long street that had once been the business district. The stores had long since been turned into antiques shops, flea markets and craft stores. Hadley's Tea Room graced a corner building and the Bluebonnet B & B next door to it catered to tourists passing through Texas Hill Country.

Essie's Diner was at the end of the two-block strip of businesses. It was next to the Farm and Feed Store, making the locals happy and the tourists charmed. The diner boasted a covered deck that overlooked the spring and the railroad tracks, where an occasional train rumbled along, blasting a horn that shook the tables.

New businesses, including a grocery store, clothing store and discount chain store, were located in a strip mall on the main road going through town.

Lucy parked up the street from the diner. She didn't allow herself to glance down the side road. She didn't want to lay eyes on her father's church. Church of the Redeemed, he'd called it.

Maria reached for her door but stopped.

"Lucy, I think Essie is trying to drag you into something you aren't going to like."

"Is that a warning?" Lucy asked as she pulled the keys from the ignition.

"Yeah, it is. It's Saturday night. Essie is closed on Saturdays."

"Then why is everyone in town?" Apprehension grew in the pit of her stomach.

"The church," Maria said. "It's new. A community thing. People meet for dinner."

"And you didn't feel the need to tell me until now?"

As Maria opened her mouth to explain, Lucy held up a hand to stop her.

"Don't worry about it. We've survived a lot. This is just stuff. We're going in. We'll have dinner with Essie. End of story."

Maria's features relaxed. "For what it's worth, I am sorry."

"It's okay. You didn't do anything, other than lure me here so you could have fried chicken."

They walked the short distance to the diner, entering to find the tables filled and conversation buzzing. Essie hurried from table to table, barely pausing to give them a distracted smile as she refilled water glasses. There were people Lucy knew, quite a few that she didn't.

A few of the locals glanced their way, quiet whispers following as they moved through the crowded dining room. Essie caught up with them.

"I have a table for you." She pointed to a table marked with a reserved sign. There were six chairs and only one was taken. By old Chet Andrews, a local farmer who had never remarried after his wife of forty years passed away. And that had been a good twenty years ago. He was dapper, with his silver hair and silver mustache. He stood up as they approached and held out a chair for Maria.

"Hello, young ladies. What a fortunate man I am, to be able to share a table with the two of you." Chet winked at Lucy as she sat across from him. "Lucy, I'm glad to see you back in Bluebonnet."

"Thank you, Chet." She reached for a menu but Maria shook her head. "No?"

Chet handed her a paper. She browsed it, her skin going clammy as she read. Essie had quietly moved away from their table.

The paper trembled in her hands as she read. The evening menu was catfish, hush puppies, fries and cole-slaw. The profit from the sales would be given to the Bluebonnet Shelter for Abused Women and Children. Located in the Community Church building. No mention of the Church of the Redeemed. The irony hit her and she laughed a little. The place that had once hidden abuse now sheltered people from it. She knew that Essie had something to do with this. She'd bought the building. She'd closed down the church her nephew had started. She'd always told Lucy that she meant to use the building to rebuild lives, not to destroy them.

A man approached. He wore an open, friendly smile on his middle-aged face. His blond hair was thinning. Laugh lines crinkled at the corners of pale gray eyes.

"Ladies, mind if I sit with you for a few minutes?"

Maria cleared her throat. "Lucy, this is Pastor Matthews."

He held out a hand to Lucy. "Pleased to meet you. I'm Duncan Matthews. Some of the residents prefer just to call me Preacher."

She took his hand briefly. "Pleased to meet you."

He sat down next to her. "I'm glad that the two of

you are here to support us. That means the world to me, and to our ministry."

"I'm not…" She started to reject the idea that she supported this ministry. A warm hand on her shoulder stopped her. She glanced up at her aunt. Essie smiled down, a gentle look in her dark eyes.

"It's a good ministry, Lucy. I told you we would find a use for that building. Pastor Mathews also started the Community Helping Hands ministry. We have teams of people. Some fix meals, others do construction work on homes that need fixing up, some do lawn work. It's a good thing. We were so glad that Duncan joined us in Bluebonnet."

"It sounds as if the church is doing a lot for the community." Lucy found the words, though her throat felt tight.

"We're trying," the pastor said. "And we'd love to have your help going forward."

"My help?" She didn't know what to say to that.

"We're remodeling, as well as trying to help prepare the women to start new lives."

"I see."

"Come by and see what we're doing."

The guy didn't back down. She gave him kudos for bravery. And with a tight smile she glanced away from the hopeful look on his face. Aunt Essie was there to distract her.

"I'll bring you a fish dinner. And I have chicken, just for Maria." Aunt Essie gave her shoulder a final pat.

Maria gave their aunt a wide smile. "Thanks, Aunt Essie."

"Anything for you, kiddo." And then she was gone.

"I'm going to step outside," Lucy said to no one in particular.

"Lucy, don't go." Maria started to stand. Of course she would insist on following if she thought Lucy meant to leave.

Lucy touched her sister's shoulder. "I'm not leaving. I just need some air. It's crowded and warm in here."

She smiled at Chet when he half stood. Quickly, ignoring people who called her name, she escaped the diner. Stepping out the side door, she inhaled the country air, a combination of spring grass, flowers and nearby farms.

She leaned against the side of the building, taking in deep breaths. Boots on the sidewalk pulled her from the quiet place where she'd found a sense of calm. She opened her eyes and groaned at the sight of the man approaching, a small child in his arms.

She stood against the building taking slow breaths. Her eyes were closed. She was whispering, counting, he thought. Dane paused, and when Issy started to speak he put a finger to her lips to quiet her. He waited a long minute as the woman standing there calmed herself, and then he took a step forward. She quickly jerked to attention and faced him.

He held up his free left hand. "I didn't mean to frighten you."

"I wasn't frightened."

No, she probably wasn't. But in that moment before she'd sensed him there, she'd looked like she was having a panic attack.

"Okay, not frightened," he conceded. He didn't know how to ask if she was okay, if she needed anything. A change of subject would probably be best. "Have you met my daughter, Isabelle?"

It worked. Lucy's features softened the tiniest bit and a hint of a smile tugged at her lips.

"I haven't. It's good to meet you, Isabelle. I've heard a lot about you."

Issy, just three years old, never feared a situation or a stranger. She held out her little hand for Lucy and grinned. "Good to meet you. I like chocolate cake."

Lucy chuckled, a little breathless. "Really? I think chocolate is my favorite, too."

"Essie always has chocolate cake. Even if it isn't my birthday."

"Does she really? Then maybe we should go inside and have a piece of cake."

"Dinner first," Dane warned his daughter.

Issy frowned and let out a loud sigh. "Dinner first."

"Are there empty chairs in there?" he asked Lucy.

"There are a few at our table."

"Is that an invitation?" Dane teased.

"Not an invitation, just a fact. Don't push it, Scott."

"Back to a last name basis? And here I thought we were friends."

A hint of a smile hovered on that wide, generous mouth of hers and she shook her head. "Neighbors."

He reached past her to push the door open and she slid through but she didn't walk away as he thought she might. Instead she walked just in front of him. If he was to guess, he thought she might need a friend. Even if she only wanted to call him a neighbor.

As she navigated the crowded café, he thought of the girl he'd known. She hadn't been a typical teen girl, eager to be seen with him, talking of forever before they'd even had a chance to know each other. She'd always been self-contained, keeping her hopes and dreams to herself.

He'd wanted desperately to know what made her tick. And then he'd wanted to protect her. He'd failed miserably on both counts.

In his arms, Issy struggled, wanting down. He leaned in close. "It's too crowded, honey."

There were too many obstacles. Too many chairs, too many legs stretched, too many purses. Born two months premature, she'd lost her vision. It had been devastating to Dane and his wife. Issy didn't know any different. She ran, she played and she chased kittens. She navigated the world with the bravery of a three-year-old.

They reached the table at the back of the room. Lucy pointed to the two remaining chairs. "I'm sure Essie reserved them for you."

Of course Essie had planned those chairs for him. Right there, next to her niece. The older woman had been telling him for over a year now that someday he'd find someone. She'd told him to give God a chance. Up to now, her meddling had been harmless.

Lucy's return to town had changed things. Essie was convinced everyone deserved a great love, the kind of love she'd shared with her husband. Dane didn't want to hurt Essie's feelings, but since his ex-wife left him, he wasn't looking for that. She hadn't been a partner in their marriage. She hadn't been a mom to Issy. The day she walked out, she said she'd never planned on being tied down on a ranch and she hadn't signed on to raise a child who was less than perfect.

He couldn't think of that day, the way she'd blindsided him, without a big dose of anger washing over him.

Essie hurried their way, her attention immediately going to Issy. "I knew you would be here. You've done so much for the church, Dane. I wanted to make sure you had a seat. And, Miss Issy, I have chocolate cake."

Dane arched a brow and Essie knew to avoid looking him in the eye. This seat had nothing to do with making sure he had a place, and everything to do with Lucy. His gaze focused on the woman standing several feet away, doing her best to ignore him.

"Don't forget me, Essie." Maria spoke up. She had a plate of chicken strips in front of her. "And if Issy doesn't want fish, I have plenty of chicken. I don't mind sharing."

He set his daughter in the chair next to Maria. Issy immediately felt for the teen, putting a hand on her cheek, then pushing up to her knees so she could get a little closer to whisper, "I like ranch dressing."

"I have it," Maria whispered back, reaching for an extra plate. "I have fries, too."

"And ketchup?" Issy patted the table and found a fork wrapped in a napkin. "Can I have chocolate milk, Miss Essie?"

Essie leaned to kiss the top of his daughter's blond head. "You sure can, Issy girl. I'll be right back. Lucy, why don't you help me get drinks? Dane will want sweet tea. Chet, what can I get you?"

"I think I've had enough." Chet leaned back and patted his rounded belly.

"Do you want pie?" Essie asked.

"Nope, can't keep a figure like this by eating pie."

Essie's hands went to her hips. "Now what kind of nonsense is that, Chet Andrews? You've been eating my pie every day for as long as I can remember. And you haven't been worrying about your boyish figure."

Chet let out a long sigh. "Doc said I have to cut back on sugar."

A waitress flitted past, saw Chet's empty coffee cup and refilled it. Chet winked at her and reached for the sugar jar but Essie moved it away from him. The maneuver earned her a scowl from the older man.

Essie didn't back down. She pointed a finger at Chet. "You put five spoons of sugar in every cup of coffee, old man. I guess it's time you put a stop to that."

"You're a hard woman, Essie." Chet lifted the cup in salute.

"Yes, well, I kind of like having you around. Even if you've never left more than a fifty-cent tip, you're a good neighbor."

Chet ignored her and sipped his coffee and grimaced. As he set the cup down he turned his attention to Lucy. "Are you back for good, Lucy?"

Dane watched her flick a glance in the direction of her younger sister, a hesitant look on her face. "I'm back for now."

It wasn't much of an answer. Not that it mattered to him. But it probably mattered a lot to her sister. A tug on his sleeve brought his attention back to the table. Issy's small hand was on his arm and she leaned close.

"Do I get cake now?" she whispered.

"Yes, you get cake." He kissed her cheek. "*After* you eat dinner."

She came up on her knees, wobbling a bit on the seat. He steadied her, making sure she was firmly planted in the middle of the chair. "Daddy, is it a party?"

"Kind of."

A hand reached past his shoulder. He glanced up as Lucy placed chocolate cake in front of his daughter. She leaned over, whispering in Issy's ear that the cake was right in front of her. With a gentleness that belied her tense expression, Lucy guided his daughter to a fork and helped her locate the cake.

Lucy Palermo was an enigma. But then again, she wasn't. There was a scar on her cheek, small and faded. She'd had that scar since the night her father caught them in town together. Another scar on her arm was more recent. He knew about the attack in Afghanistan.

There'd been years of abuse and no one in town had stepped in to stop it. His own family had been guilty of turning a blind eye to the problems on the ranch next door. His dad hadn't wanted to get involved. His mom had commented that it was a shame and Mrs. Palermo should have taken the kids with her when she left.

Lucy started to step away but her gaze caught his. He schooled his features with an easy smile. Lucy froze, her dark eyes holding his captive. Finally she shook her head, as if shaking free from memories.

As she walked away he had an uncharacteristic thought, one that had nothing to do with the past and everything to do with the present. But their history belonged firmly in the past. It had been a summer romance that ended with casualties.

They were different people now. She had come home with more scars. He had his own scars and his own motivations for making wiser choices. They were both wounded, and in this situation two halves didn't add up to a whole. Instead it would just be two broken people making a mess of not just their lives, but the lives of the people who counted on them.

But there were certain things he couldn't deny. She still looked good in jeans. And she could still get his attention with a look.

Chapter Four

Lucy walked down Main Street, enjoying the quiet spring morning. It was Monday and Bluebonnet was peaceful, with few cars parked along the narrow street and businesses just opening up. She stopped in front of Lawson's Five and Dime. The department store had been a mainstay in this tiny town since the early 1900s, and it had been a mainstay in Lucy's life for as long as she could remember. Mrs. Lawson, the fourth Mrs. Lawson to stand behind the counter of the store with free gum for every child, had been a favorite of Lucy's.

Harriet Lawson had attended the Church of the Redeemed. But she hadn't stayed long. She'd stood up to Jesse Palermo, calling him out for his treatment of his family.

Saturday evening at the diner she'd given a moving speech about the new Community Church and shelter, talking about lives being changed for the better and women finding freedom from abuse. The irony hadn't been lost on Lucy. A church that had once destroyed was now in the business of rebuilding.

A movement inside the building caught her attention. She saw Mrs. Lawson move through the shop.

The older woman waved and smiled big as she hurried toward the door, waving keys in silent communication. Lucy hadn't planned on talking. She'd just been lost in thought and she'd stood there too long.

Keys turned in the lock and the door opened. Mrs. Lawson, short dark hair, an apron over her jeans and T-shirt, stepped out on the sidewalk and pulled her into a hug that Lucy had no way to pull free from.

"Lucy Palermo, it's so good to see you back in town. And I was so thrilled to see you at the dinner Saturday evening." She let go and stepped back from the hug. "Come inside. I just put on a pot of coffee."

Lucy glanced around. "I just had breakfast at Essie's."

"Oh, come on. You aren't here by chance. You have questions."

Did she?

Mrs. Lawson motioned her inside the store. Lucy followed and she couldn't help but inhale the familiar scent of polished wood, the favorite perfumes of every woman in town, and something distinctly cinnamon.

The aisles were still crowded, the lights were still too dim, and because she'd grown up, the store seemed smaller than it had to the little girl Lucy had once been. She followed Mrs. Lawson down one of those narrow aisles cluttered with dishes that had been on sale since Lucy's childhood. No one seemed to want the harvest gold ceramic ware.

Lucy could smell freshly brewed coffee. Mrs. Lawson motioned her inside an office with dark green furniture and a ceiling fan that clicked as it circulated stale air.

"Have a seat." She pointed to a chair. "Sugar in your coffee? And I have snickerdoodles. I know they're not an acceptable breakfast food but I baked them for the ladies at the shelter and couldn't resist."

"Black coffee and I'd love a cookie." She didn't really want to talk about the shelter. She knew it was coming, though. Mrs. Lawson was giving her those quick, covert looks, as if she expected her to bolt any second.

Once they had their coffee, Mrs. Lawson settled herself at the desk. She finished off a cookie, wiping crumbs from the front of her shirt, and then she settled her well-meaning gaze on Lucy.

"You've done well for yourself," Mrs. Lawson said. "I always worried about you kids. I should have done more after I left the church but I just didn't know what to do. When your mom left, I thought she'd take you kids with her. I guess I shouldn't have been surprised when she didn't."

"Water under the bridge," Lucy said. She eyed the exit, wishing she could escape the store and this conversation. Who would stop her?

Mrs. Lawson reached out, as if she meant to stop her. But she drew her hand back and settled in her chair.

She reached for another cookie. "Lucy, I don't have a right to give you advice. Except that I feel somewhat responsible. In the beginning we followed your father and his teachings. I'm not sure how we were so gullible. I look back and can't fathom that I would be pulled in to something so wrong. But it was wrong. It was destructive. It left people shattered. Including you kids. That's one reason we're all so thankful for Pastor Matthews and his vision for that church. The new ministry helps people escape abusive situations. It lifts people up, the way God intended. I'd like for you to visit because I want you to experience God and not the false gospel your father preached."

Lucy set her coffee cup on the desk and stood to go. But she wouldn't walk away angry, because Mrs. Lawson had the best intentions. She knew, better than anyone, what the Palermos had been through. She'd been through it, too.

"Lucy, I'm sorry. I guess I've overstepped."

"No, you didn't. I know you mean to help. I know the new church is trying to do the same. But I'm not here to be a part of this church. I'm not even planning to stay in Bluebonnet."

"I'm sorry to hear that. But I hope you'll at least stop by the church."

Lucy paused at the door. "I appreciate you talking to me. And I will stop by the church."

She left the five-and-dime and headed for her truck, done with town, with well-meaning friends, with long, questioning looks from locals who weren't sure about her.

As she headed out of town, she took a right turn. She hadn't really planned to go by the church but curiosity was stronger than her best intentions. She wanted to see what had happened to the building, the ministry and the people she had known. Mrs. Lawson was an example of people who had moved on. They hadn't allowed her father's ministry to determine their future. Or they had, but in a positive way. They were giving back rather than holding themselves back.

Lucy had always held herself back, except for that one summer with Dane when she'd really allowed herself to feel. She'd always been an outsider, the child on the edge of the playground, the adult at the edge of social groups. She'd been trained from early on not to talk, not to share, to let no one in. She realized now that her father had done that to them, not to protect them, but to protect himself.

The church building was L shaped. There was the main sanctuary with a bell tower. The double doors of the vestibule faced the street. A wing added on when she was a child was attached to the back of the main sanctuary. As she pulled up there were a few women working in the flower gardens. A man on a ladder was repairing roof gutters.

Suddenly the women stopped working. They watched her as she pulled into a parking space. She couldn't see their expressions but from their body language she knew they were nervous, maybe fearful. One of the ladies ran back inside, using the side door of the building. The man on the ladder descended.

An old beat-up truck pulled in next to hers. The man getting out was thin. His hair was shoulder length. He hadn't shaved in a while but the beard didn't hide the pasty complexion of a drug addict or the scars on his face.

He approached the man who had gotten off the ladder. She recognized him from the benefit at Essie's. Pastor Matthews didn't look like a man who backed down easily. He also didn't appear to need her help. But she got out of her truck and headed his way, anyway.

"I'm here to get my wife," the newcomer shouted. He headed past the pastor but a shoulder check kept him from getting too far.

"I'm sorry, but I'm going to have to ask you to leave," Pastor Matthews said with a semblance of gentility.

"My wife is here with my kid and I want her to come home."

"Sir, I'm sorry but you'll have to leave. If you have

a wife who wants to come home, I'm sure she'll get in touch with you."

"Willa, get out here! Get Seth. We're going home. Come on now, honey. You know I didn't mean to hit you."

Lucy shook her head. She'd heard that too many times in her life. She could hear her father's voice, telling her if she'd just done what she knew was right, he wouldn't have had to hit her.

It had always been her fault, her mom's fault, the fault of her brothers. Jesse Palermo had never once meant he was sorry for his behavior. He'd only been sorry they hadn't lived up to his standards.

"What are you looking at?" the man shouted, his attention now on Lucy.

She shrugged. "Not much."

With a growl, he came at her. Maybe that's what she'd wanted, to show him that not all women could be beat down. As he charged her, she readied herself, focusing, then struck out. With two moves she had him pinned to the ground, begging for mercy, then threatening to get her for this. She smiled and asked him how he planned on doing that.

Pastor Matthews put a hand on her shoulder. "I think you can let him go." He leaned over to look at the man on the ground. "You're going to go home now. Correct?"

"Yeah, I'll leave. But Willa is going to come home with me."

"I don't think she wants to."

"No, I'll go." A quiet voice came from behind Lucy.

Lucy released the man. She stood to face the petite young woman, a toddler in her arms. She still wore the black eye she'd probably gotten from her husband.

"Don't."

Willa shrugged. "He's my man."

"He isn't a man," Lucy responded, giving him a look. "Real men don't hit women."

"I'll show you a real man." He came at her again but Lucy held a hand up and at least he had the good sense to know this wasn't a fight he would win.

"Willa, please think about the safety of your child." It wasn't any of Lucy's business.

But isn't that what people had probably said about her family? For years no one had gotten involved. Every now and then a teacher had questioned a mark or a bruise. She'd always had an explanation. She'd been breaking a horse, fixing fence, working on the barn. This woman probably had plenty of excuses, too.

"He won't hurt us anymore. You're sorry, ain't you, Johnny?"

Johnny shot her a pleased look and moved in next to her. "You know I am, Willa. Sometimes you just don't know when to shut up and you make me so mad. But we're better now, aren't we?"

Willa nodded her head and Johnny put an arm around her and headed her toward the truck. Lucy took a step after them but a hand on her arm stopped her.

"You can't make them stay." Pastor Matthews spoke quietly, words of reason she wanted to deny. She wanted to make Willa stay.

"No, you can't," she agreed as she watched Johnny help Willa and his son into the truck.

"I'm surprised to see you here," the pastor said as they watched the truck ease down the driveway. Once it hit the road, Johnny gunned the engine and flew past the church, honking the horn and yelling.

"You invited me to come take a look," she said. He had issued the invitation at the diner on Saturday.

"Yes, I did." He motioned toward the building. "I'll give you a tour. And maybe you'll decide to do more than look. We can always use an extra hand around here. We definitely don't have anyone who can deliver a right punch the way you just did."

She looked up, saw humor in his expression and relaxed a bit. "I do have an unusual skill set. But I'm not here because I want to volunteer."

"I'm sorry to hear that. If you change your mind, you know where to find us."

"Yes, I do."

"So we'll start with a tour?"

She studied the building, seeing so much of the past but seeing the new, as well. A coward would make excuses. She had to get home. There were fences to fix. She had a sister who probably wondered where she'd gone. But deep down she knew she needed to face this building. She had to face her past.

She would walk through the building, compliment what they were trying to do and never return.

They started in the sanctuary. The carpet had been pulled up and old hardwood floors refinished. The pews were new. The pulpit her father had stood behind was gone. Sunlight filtered through amber-colored windows, bathing the sanctuary in golden warmth. She could hear hammering at the back of the church and the hum of conversation from behind the building.

She could also hear her father's words, taking well-known Bible verses and bending them to his will and purpose. Women should be quiet. Children should obey. Always used as an excuse to keep them in line, to beat them into submission.

The twins. Her brothers. She smiled, thinking of the difficulty their father'd had trying to bend their will to his. The more he beat them, the more determined they were to oppose him.

Lucy was the opposite. She'd built a shell, remained quiet, took the abuse until she could leave.

A hand touched her arm. "Are you okay?"

She nodded, aware that she had half hugged herself as she stood there staring up at the pulpit. *Words can never hurt you.* She reminded herself of the old adage, meant to keep children from being hurt by bullies.

Words. Words took pieces from an already-broken heart, ripped at a wounded soul and left scars no one could see.

Words would always hurt.

Her vision narrowed as she took another deep breath. "I have to go."

Pastor Matthews offered her a grim smile. "Too much?"

She focused her sight on the door, her escape route. Always know where the exits are, a safety tip they stressed in their bodyguard business. "I think so. I do appreciate what you're trying to do here."

"If you need us, we're here."

"I'm good but thank you." Her vision clouded as she hurried through those double doors at the front of the church.

She ran straight into Dane Scott as he was coming up the steps of the church. "Whoa."

His hands steadied her.

She blinked back tears. She didn't cry. She *wouldn't* cry. Instead she brushed off his hands and kept walking. If she had any sense left at all she would get in her truck and head back to Austin and a job that would keep her mind busy.

She stopped midway to her truck, bending at the

waist, taking deep breaths to ease the tension in her lungs. A hand on her back rubbed slow circles. She shook her head but he wouldn't leave. Why wouldn't he leave?

"Take slow breaths." His voice rumbled close to her ear.

"Go away," she rasped out, trying but not quite managing to sound like herself.

He laughed. "That's the Lucy we all know and love."

"Take a hike, Scott."

"Right. As soon as I make sure you're not going to pass out on the church steps."

She stiffened beneath his touch. "I don't pass out."

"Of course you don't."

"Neighbors don't get in a person's business. You are getting in my business." She still couldn't look at him.

"Yeah, I guess that must mean we're friends. Everyone needs friends." He stood close, his shoulder against hers. She'd felt chilled but his nearness brought a warmth. Someone recently had told her everyone needed human touch. Of course she'd debated the fact.

"I have friends," she argued. She nearly thanked him for the disagreement. Anything to take her mind off the panic that had edged in.

"Look, if it makes you happy, I'm not thrilled with the idea of friendship. Really. You're not pleasant. You rarely stick around. Not exactly the best qualities in a friend. But here we are."

"You obviously can't take a hint."

"Rarely," he said in a teasing voice that made her smile. Not a full smile, though. She wouldn't give him that.

Instead she moved away from his hand that was all too comforting. "I have to go."

"Of course you do."

She faced him, noticing the teasing glint in his too-blue eyes.

"I think I've proven that I'm not quite ready to go in there. And seriously, Dane Scott, if this gets out, I'm coming after you."

"You mean if people find out you're human?" He winked. "We wouldn't want the whole world to know that, would we?"

"No, we wouldn't. I've worked hard at…" What had she meant to say? And why was she saying anything to him? Because he was easy to talk to, she remembered. She'd made that discovery at sixteen, telling him everything she'd never planned on telling anyone. "I've worked hard at letting go and moving on."

The teasing glint faded from his eyes and was replaced with something softer, warmer. "Sometimes facing our fears makes us stronger."

She wanted to hurt him. Really, was he going to be tender? Like she was his young daughter waking up from a bad dream?

She didn't want tenderness. Or sympathy. She backed away from him. "Fine, I'll go back inside. But I don't need you there to hold my hand."

He held up both hands. "I wouldn't dream of it. *Friend.*"

"Neighbor," she mumbled as she walked away.

Dane followed Lucy inside the church. He shouldn't have. He should have gotten back to work. He was planning on replacing light fixtures in the dorms that had been created in the old Sunday school rooms. Instead he walked behind her, ignoring the tense set of her shoulders and the fact that she didn't want him along for this journey.

He couldn't stop himself, though. Even with her quills up, Lucy had an easy way about her. She had a sense of humor, an easy smile, and she was kind. They were parts of her personality she didn't seem comfortable with. He shouldn't be comfortable with them, either, because those parts drew him to her, and that was the last thing he needed.

"Stop thinking about me." She shot the comment over her shoulder as she walked through the kitchen. "I'm not a project. I don't need to be fixed. Go do whatever good deed you were going to do here today, Dane."

He stepped next to her as she stood, surveying the homey kitchen Pastor Matthews and his wife, Amy, had created in this church. "I'm replacing light fixtures and repairing some sockets. You're not on my 'to do' list."

"Thank goodness for that," she said as she kept walking. "The kitchen is nice."

"Yes, it is."

"I'm glad this church is being used this way. Definitely not what my father would have wanted."

"It's a good ministry and they are having some success helping women to get out of abusive situations. They also try to find counseling for the husbands."

"There are always going to be women who won't walk away from the abuse."

"That's true," he stated.

"Life doesn't come with guarantees. Or maybe there is one. We all have our baggage. You included." She shot him a look.

"Yeah," he agreed. "Me included."

"Issy's mom?"

"She left when Issy was a year old. Fortunately my daughter won't remember her mother walking out on us."

"No, she won't. But you will." She stopped and faced him. "She has you, Dane. That's more than a lot of kids have."

"Yeah, she has me." But that hadn't been the plan. He'd considered himself a part of a couple. Only to learn he wasn't, and now he was a single dad.

He led her to the nursery that also served as a make-shift day care. There were two little girls playing with blocks as one of the older church members, Mrs. Gilly, watched over them.

"Their moms either have jobs or are out finding jobs, if they can," Dane explained to Lucy as she glanced around the brightly painted room. "Ladies from church volunteer to watch their children."

She watched the children play, tossed a quick nod to Mrs. Gilly, then she left. Dane followed her into the hall and didn't ask if she was okay. He already knew the answer and knew she wouldn't want to admit out loud that she felt as if she was coming apart on the inside.

He led her down the hall to the living area. It was empty other than a big gray cat sprawled on the window seat. She approached the long-haired feline and, with her gaze focused on a distant hill, she ran a hand down the animal's back.

"I should go now. Maria will wonder if I've left the county." She glanced back at him. "With good reason. Since I've done it before. And since our mother does it on a regular basis."

"I think you had good reason for leaving," he offered.

The cat stood, stretched and brushed against her hand. "Maybe, but now I need to be here. Did you ever consider leaving?"

"I went to college, got a degree and came home to run the ranch. My folks moved to Dallas soon after. Dad has Parkinson's."

She nodded, because of course she knew all of that. "I'm not sure why we keep our ranch," she admitted with a slight shrug. Then she headed for the door that led outside and he followed. "Mom obviously doesn't want it. The boys are too busy riding bulls. I haven't wanted to be here."

"The twins will grow up, and then they'll feel differently. You might feel differently."

The sun beat down on them as they stood on the patio. It was May and it was already miserably hot. The woman standing next to him didn't seem to notice. She pushed the sunglasses off the top of her head and positioned them to cover her eyes.

"Yes, maybe I'll feel differently someday." Lucy glanced at her watch. "I have to go. Thank you for the tour."

"You're welcome. I'll walk you to your truck."

She gave him a hard stare. "I don't need an escort to my truck."

"No, you don't. I offered because I want to walk you to your truck."

She pulled back a bit, and he knew he'd messed up.

"No," she repeated. "I appreciate the tour and it was nice to catch up."

He got it. She was giving him the brush-off. "Lucy, you don't have to worry. I'm not looking to start anything."

"Good to know," she said. "So, I'll walk myself to my truck."

He tipped his hat, conceding something that felt a bit like defeat. That was the last thing he expected to feel as she walked away.

Chapter Five

Lucy grabbed a bag of grain off the back of her truck and carried it into the feed room. When she walked back out of the stable, Maria was waiting for her. The youngest Palermo was leaning against the truck, a hand on her belly, the warm Texas breeze blowing her hair.

It was Thursday and after nearly a week home, they were falling into a routine. Lucy made frequent trips to town for supplies. Maria thought about food. A lot.

"Did you bring me lunch?" Maria asked. The poodle ran out from under the truck and started to yap.

Lucy pointed at the dog and he plopped to the ground, whimpering as he buried his nose in his paws. Maria looked from the dog to Lucy and back to the dog.

"How did you do that?"

Lucy shrugged. "I'm mean. And yeah, I did bring you lunch. How are you feeling?"

"Horrible. Did Aunt Essie tell you that they're having a workday Saturday? At the church?"

"No. Should she have told me?"

"I guess not. I just thought she might have mentioned it. I plan on going. I usually help out in the nursery. Dane feels better if I'm with Issy. He has a hard time leaving her." As she talked, Maria rummaged in the truck finding the to-go container from the café. She lifted the lid and inhaled before heading to sit on the bench at the side of the stable.

Calling it a stable seemed a bit of a stretch. The metal building had stalls, storage rooms and an attached outdoor arena. But there were pieces of sheet metal missing from the roof, compliments of last year's too-close-for-comfort tornado.

She eyed her sister, sitting with the foam container on her lap. Maria grinned as she dug into Essie's homemade enchiladas.

"Oh, by the way, Dane is bringing Issy over for me to babysit her."

"Why?" Lucy grabbed another feed sack and headed for the door.

"I told you. I babysit her. You don't listen."

Lucy carried the feed sack inside, dumped it in the feed room and headed back outside. She sat down next to Maria.

"I listen. You said Dane trusts you with Issy. You didn't mention watching her today."

"Oh, sorry." Maria shoved another bite of food into her mouth. "We were talking about the church."

"Right, and how you volunteer in the nursery."

Maria nodded, but then turned a bit green. She jumped up, hand to her mouth, and ran for the bathroom at the other end of the stable.

Lucy followed, the poodle keeping step with her, barking and yipping the entire time, its long, gray curls looking the worse for having rolled in something less than pleasant on the ranch. Maria was sitting on the dirt floor of the stable, head resting on knees that were drawn to her chest.

Lucy sank down next to her. She put an awkward arm around her younger sister and drew her close. They weren't an affectionate family, she realized as they sat there together. She couldn't remember their parents ever hugging. The closest they'd come to affection had been the nights Maria had crawled into bed with Lucy.

"So, we need to make a doctor's appointment." Lucy repeated what their aunt had told her. "And we need to eat healthier."

"Did you buy a pregnancy book?" Maria asked as she leaned in close.

"Aunt Essie texted me a list," Lucy admitted. "Are you drinking plenty of water?"

"I'm drinking water. Actually I do have a book."

They sat in silence for a while. The poodle crawled onto Maria's lap and dozed. Birds swooped through the stable, building nests on support beams.

"I'm sorry," Maria whispered against Lucy's shoulder.

"For what?"

Maria shrugged but didn't move out of Lucy's embrace.

"For everything. For getting pregnant. For dragging you away from your life. I know you don't want to be here. If Mom had stayed…"

"Don't apologize. We'll figure this out."

"I know, but this is the last place you want to be," Maria continued, forcing Lucy to have a conversation she wanted to avoid.

Lucy took a deep breath and nodded. Her sister knew, so there was no use lying. Not to herself or to Maria.

"It's the last place I wanted to be. But it's the only place I would choose to be right now." She shrugged. "It is surprisingly not horrible."

Maria pulled away from her. "At least you're not getting all warm and fuzzy. If you did, then I would really start to worry."

"No need to worry about me being warm and fuzzy." Lucy stood and held a hand out to pull Maria to her feet.

As they walked back out into bright sunlight, a truck pulled down the drive and parked. Maria giggled just a little.

"You carved his name in your dresser, didn't you?" Maria asked.

"It was a lifetime ago. But yeah, when I was young and foolish."

Dane helped Issy out of the truck, and then headed their way.

"End of conversation," Lucy warned.

Maria zipped her lips but the twinkle in her eyes said this was far from over.

"Dane, I didn't expect you this early," Maria said.

Dane hefted a bag over his arm, a frilly pink bag with flowers and lace. He held Issy's hand and she navigated the turf with careful steps. Her smile was bright and her sweet face was framed in unruly blond curls.

"If you don't mind a few extra hours, I need to drive up to Killeen for some supplies for the shelter." He looked down at his little girl. "If it's too much, Issy can go with me."

"Of course it isn't a problem," Maria answered. Lucy wanted to chime in that it *was* a problem.

She'd come home for her sister but she hadn't expected to get dragged back into small town life. She hadn't expected Dane. Or a little girl with blond curls and a captivating smile. She definitely hadn't expected to remember why she'd carved Dane's name in her dresser.

This was not the nice, neat package she liked to call life. This was messy. She didn't do messy.

Dane cleared his throat, jerking her attention back to him, to the questioning look in his eyes. The corner of his mouth tilted up ever so slightly. Fear tangled up inside her, because she didn't know what was more intimidating, the little girl or her father.

"Is it a problem?" He left the question dangling.

"Of course not." She glanced back at Maria already taking Issy by the hand and leading her to the house. It seemed that her little sister was more than up for this job. Lucy would rather be on a security detail. A job that seemed far less intimidating than caring for a small child.

"She's a great babysitter so you shouldn't have to worry about a thing."

"I'm not worried. Do I look worried?"

He laughed, his eyes crinkling at the corners. "Yes, Lucy, you look worried."   .

"Well, I'm not." She could handle a tiny person being in their home.

He glanced at his watch. "I'll try not to be gone too long. Also, I'm buying a security system for the shelter. Pastor Matthews wanted me to ask if you have any suggestions."

"I've helped to install a few systems. I can do a little research and text you the information."

"Thank you. And would you help install it Saturday?"

That's the way a person got dragged in. Because she couldn't say no. She couldn't tell them that she wasn't interested in their church or the shelter. Protection was her business. And protecting the women at the shelter was important.

"I'll help."

"Thank you."

Lucy watched as he drove away, and then she headed for the house. She found Maria and Issy inside. They were sitting on the living room floor stacking blocks. Issy giggled when Maria handed her a block and said, "Oh, this is red. It's hot."

The block tumbled from tiny hands. Maria replaced it with a blue one. "This is blue. It's cold."

Issy tossed the block and yelled that her hands were freezing. The dog started to bark and Lucy pointed, sending the animal back to his dog bed.

"Want to play with us, Lucy?" Maria asked, sprawling on the floor like an overgrown kid. Lucy guessed that wasn't far from the truth.

"I have to feed, but then I'll come in and we'll play."

"Issy and I like to dance," Maria offered, because she knew that Lucy didn't have a clue. She'd had younger siblings but as an adult she'd had little interaction with children.

They frightened her. She didn't want to admit that. She didn't want to admit that she thought they were breakable. They were also unpredictable.

To prove that point, Issy was on her feet and heading Lucy's direction, little hands grasping her as she got close. She picked the child up and Issy brushed hands across her face.

"She likes you," Maria said in wonder.

"I'm not *that* bad." Lucy spoke softly as little hands tangled in her hair and the child's forehead touched hers.

Dane's child. She closed her eyes and held the little girl close for a few seconds longer than she'd intended.

"No, you're not that bad. You do act as if you've never held a child before."

"I've held a child. One, actually." Her business partner, Daron McKay's stepdaughter, Jamie. "I have to head back to the barn now and get some work done."

Maria saluted. "Are you taking Issy with you?"

Taking Issy with her? She still held the child in her arms and Issy smiled, as if she knew the answer would be in her favor. She leaned close to Lucy's ear. "Do you have a pony?"

"No, we don't. But I think we have kittens. Do you want to see the kittens?"

Issy looked a little lost. "I can't see the kittens."

"No, but we can touch them and feel their noses."

"Noses are wet." Issy seemed proud of that observation.

"Yes, sometimes they are."

"Okay, we'll see the kittens." Issy's arms went around her neck and held tight. "And ride a pony."

Lucy didn't bother arguing about ponies. Dane would be home soon and the pony argument could be his to lose. As they walked toward the barn she noticed movement along the fence. It didn't look like a dog or even a coyote. It looked like a person cowering, crawling and believing they were out of sight. Unfortunately she had Issy in her arms and she wasn't about to go after them in the growing darkness and with a child on her hip.

The sun had long set when Dane pulled up to the Palermo ranch. A light glowed yellow in the living room window. He glanced at the digital clock on the dash. It was an hour past Issy's bedtime. He rolled his shoulders as he sat there in his truck. The gesture didn't do much to relieve the tension that had been building in his shoulder blades.

He forced himself to get out and head for the front

door. As he climbed the steps he saw them through the sheer living room curtains. Issy and Lucy curled up on the sofa. His daughter was sound asleep, her mouth slightly open and one arm plopped over the side of the couch. The poodle slept on the floor but close to her hand.

Lucy was awake, her eyes on the door, waiting.

He didn't knock, but instead quietly eased the door open and stepped inside. As he did, Lucy slid away from Issy and came to her feet. She put a finger to her lips as she moved away from the couch. Dane waited by the front door, unsure of what he should do. Lucy motioned him forward, gesturing toward the kitchen. He followed, with a quick look at his still-sleeping child.

The large country kitchen was lit with a single light above the sink. A lot of cleaning had been done since the last time he'd been in the house. It smelled clean. The counters were free of clutter. The biggest change was the woman leaning against the counter, her dark hair pulled back in a ponytail, her eyes wary as she shifted away from him, to fill the coffeepot with water.

"Are you okay?" she asked, her tone cool, matter-of-fact.

He might have guessed that she didn't care, so cool was her tone. But there was warmth in her eyes, in the quick look she gave him as she started the coffee.

"Yes, I'm good. Sorry it took so long. I had to make several stops to get the equipment. Thank you for that text, it did help. And then when I got back, we had a water issue at the church."

She crossed her arms in front of her and studied his face. "That expression is troubled."

"A little." Without asking, he pulled two mugs out of the cabinet.

It was the most domestic moment he could remember since before his daughter's birth.

The thought took him by surprise as he watched Lucy reach into a cabinet for cookies, the package already open. It wasn't a difficult thing, watching her move around a kitchen. She was quiet, not the type to fill the silence with empty words. Instead she took a couple of cookies and offered the package to him.

"So?" she prodded.

"I got a call from my ex-wife. First time she's called in over a year."

"Does she want something?" she finally responded as she was pouring coffee into the two cups.

"I'm not sure."

He followed her to the table at the end of the room. The poodle joined them, jumping onto a chair and watching intently as they ate cookies. Lucy tossed the dog a small piece and then she waited, watching Dane as if she expected him to tell her everything.

He couldn't remember the last time he'd talked about Tamara to anyone. Issy rarely asked about the mother she didn't know or miss. His family and friends didn't mention the wife who had walked out on him.

Every now and then someone, usually one of the older ladies at church, would ask him if he planned on remarrying. Because they thought he would want a wife and more children. He'd never planned on being a divorced father of one. It had just become who he was. He and Issy were a team. He'd avoided dating because if a child's mother walked away, he wasn't going to put other women in her life who might do the same.

"Do you want another cookie?" Lucy pushed the package across the table.

"Thanks," he said, snatching two. "She wanted me to

know she's remarried. And pregnant. She asked about Issy."

"Does she want to see her?"

"She didn't mention a visit. She said she wants to keep a line of communication open. After all, Issy is going to be a big sister. Those were her words."

They sat in silence for a few minutes. He thought maybe the personal conversation might have been more than Lucy had expected. She didn't know Tamara. And for a dozen years she hadn't really known him.

"Who knew this would be us as adults," she finally said.

"What did you expect?"

She dipped a cookie in her coffee and shrugged. "I thought of myself far away from here. I pictured you married and raising kids. I'm sorry it didn't work out."

He stretched and beneath the table his foot brushed hers. He hadn't meant for that to happen. Maybe if he'd been a few years younger, less jaded, less cautious. And maybe if the woman sitting across from him didn't have that shuttered look in her eyes.

Maybe if she was a woman who had any intention of sticking around.

"More coffee?" she asked, surprising him. He thought she'd be in a hurry to show them the door.

"I'll get it." He took her cup with his to refill them.

As he poured the coffee she moved from her seat, surprising him when she joined him.

"Dane, I'm not good at this."

"Good at what?" he asked as he handed her the cup of coffee.

She leaned against the counter, her gaze drifting away from him. "I'm not the person people generally turn to when they need to confide."

He nodded, hiding the smile she wouldn't have appreciated. "I understand. And I'll confess, I don't usually spill everything."

That earned him her full attention, dark eyes meeting his, not wavering or looking away. "I'm glad you told me. After all, we're neighbors."

He cut her off with a grin. "Friends."

She rolled her eyes. "Neighbors."

"Right." He took a step closer, bridging the distance between them. Her dark eyes clashing with his. There was a warning in them. One he should heed if he had any sense at all.

He wasn't a complete fool. He knew she could knock him to the ground in a matter of seconds, probably break his arm if she wanted, so he proceeded with caution. He set his cup down on the counter but kept his hands to himself as he leaned in and touched his lips to hers. He gave her a second to object. When she didn't, he touched her back and pulled her closer, taking his time the way a man ought to. She brought both hands up to his shoulders, and instead of clinging there, she pushed him back. Her dark eyes snapped with anger.

"No."

He closed his eyes at the word, because he should have been telling himself the same thing. "I'm sorry."

"Of course you are," she said so matter-of-factly he had to see if she looked as composed as she sounded. She did.

"I'm not sorry I kissed you," he insisted.

"You will be. Tomorrow you'll wake up and wonder what you were thinking. You'll realize that a kiss between us complicates everything. I don't want complications. I don't want regrets."

He brushed a hand through his hair, conceding to her rationale. "You're right."

"I know I am," she said with conviction and the slightest hint of humor. "I can't afford any mistakes right now."

"Daddy?" The frightened cry brought him back to his senses.

"I'm here, Issy." He walked away from Lucy.

She followed. He'd known she would. But he had to get to Issy. She wasn't used to waking up in a strange place. At home she slept in a nursery attached to his room. The path between her room and his was free of clutter.

She stood next to the couch she'd been sleeping on, her little hand holding tight to the cushion, her bunny in her other hand. The poodle stood next to her.

"I'm here, Issy." He reached for her and she flung herself into his arms. "It's okay, sweetie. I'm here."

She nodded against his shoulder, her hand coming up to touch his cheek, reassuring herself in the way she'd always done.

"Lucy made macaroni," she whispered in his ear. "It was homemade."

"Was it? And did you like it?"

She giggled. "It's better than yours. And she had cookies."

"I can't believe hers are better than mine."

His daughter belly laughed. "She even told me a story."

"Did she?" He looked at the woman who said she dealt in facts, not emotion. He hated to tell her that his child and a kiss had blown her cover. Possibly for good.

Lucy Palermo might want to deny it, but she had a

heart. A very decent heart. She might not wear it on her sleeve but it existed.

Lucy tilted her head. "I have my own recipe. If you're nice, I'll share."

"I'll be nice," he agreed. "Can you help me tomorrow? Pastor Matthews is in a hurry to get the security system installed at the shelter."

"I'll help." She acted as if she wanted to say more. When he gave her a pointed look, inviting her to say whatever was on her mind, she shook her head. "Some other time."

"If you change your mind, you have my number."

He gathered up his daughter and Lucy followed them to his truck, carrying Issy's bag, filled with dolls, books and blocks. She stood nearby as he buckled Issy into her seat. Without a word she handed him the bag and took a step back as he closed the back door of the truck. The moon was full and bathed the farm in its silvery light. The barn and house were silhouettes against the dark backdrop of the sky. In the distance a coyote howled.

Lucy turned to go but he stopped her.

She shook her head at his hand touching hers.

"Still friends?" he asked.

"Neighbors," she insisted. "Nothing has changed."

He let go of her hand, then watched as she hurried back to the house. As the door closed with a firm thud, he got in his truck and drove away. She was right to put him in his place. He'd been wrong to kiss her. He'd gotten carried away in the moment.

The fact that it had felt like the most *right* thing he'd experienced in a long time was something he'd have to think about later.

Chapter Six

Lucy left the house early the next morning. Maria had still been in bed. She'd mumbled that she didn't want to wake up. Ever. But she'd asked for food. Lucy had tossed her a package of soda crackers and promised something from Essie's for lunch.

As she drove down the highway toward town, she noticed a car turning onto the driveway that led to the Scott ranch. As she got closer she could read the sign on the side of the car. Big Country Realty.

It was none of her business.

She didn't need to know what Dane Scott was doing with his ranch. And maybe it was just a visitor. Someone from town going out to look at cattle. Maybe a friend of Haven's.

He wouldn't sell the ranch.

She turned on the radio to a country station. She didn't care what Dane was up to. What mattered to her was Maria and the ranch. No, he definitely did not matter.

For years, Don't Get Involved was her motto. It served her well. It kept her head in the game when it came to the protection business. Staying detached kept her focused.

But something had happened, because she was more involved than she'd been in years. She couldn't—wouldn't—walk away. Not from Maria. Not from the ranch.

An image flashed through her mind of a smiling little girl with blond ringlets. Issy Scott. Dane's daughter was hard to resist. Lucy couldn't imagine a mother walking away from that little girl.

She turned the radio up louder and focused hard on the road, because she wasn't going to get emotional. She wasn't going to allow herself to think about a mom who would walk away, the same way her own mom had.

That wasn't what all moms did. They stayed and protected. They nurtured. They taught their girls to be strong.

She forced herself to sing along with George Strait as she drove through Bluebonnet. Because she wasn't getting involved. She wasn't.

She pulled into the parking lot of the church and realized she was a fraud. She was very much involved. Last night she'd cuddled on the couch with Dane's daughter and sang her songs she remembered from childhood, from days that had been a little easier, sweeter. Today she was volunteering at a women's shelter.

All signs of someone losing control of the thin thread of self-preservation.

Pastor Matthews met her at the front of the church. He was carrying a ladder but he managed a quick wave.

"Lucy, what a surprise. A blessing, actually."

"I don't know that I've ever been called a blessing."

He laughed. "Most compliments are said behind a person's back. A shame, really, because we should tell people when they've done something to enrich our lives. You're definitely a blessing if you're here to help with the security system."

"I am," she answered. She must have sounded hesitant because he shot her a quick look, quirking one brow in question.

She didn't respond. She was there—that was what mattered.

"The system is in my office. I'd hoped we could take our time and hire someone to install it, but with the problems we've had, that isn't an option."

"Problems?"

He leaned the ladder against the side of the building and started to climb, pulling vines from the siding. "A husband or two intent on causing trouble."

"Is there anything I can do to help with that?" she asked, reaching to hold the ladder that swayed with his movements.

"The security system is going to be a great help." He yanked the last weed and climbed back down. "Dane's here. He's an electrical genius. He offered to help with wiring."

Dane joined them as they were walking toward the back side entrance of the church. There was an awkward moment when he looked at her and she felt heat crawl up her neck. Last night had been a breach of her well-armed defense system. He'd caught her at a weak moment.

Today she was back in control.

"Problem?" he asked as he stepped to the side and motioned her through the door.

"Not at all," she responded.

They entered through the kitchen door. There were

women inside and what appeared to be a cooking class was taking place. Pastor Matthews greeted the women.

"We try to have classes here at the church. Cooking, budgeting, easy repairs. We're getting computers hooked up in a few weeks and we'll have courses available."

"You're doing a great job." Dane thumped the pastor on the back. "This is exactly what we envisioned for the church."

Lucy stopped midstride, her attention caught by the cautious look given her by one of the women in the kitchen. The other woman stopped midsentence as she was explaining how to make something with egg whites.

"Marsha Tucker?" Lucy asked, aware that Dane was standing near her right shoulder.

His presence shouldn't have made her feel stronger. Or more secure. She was Lucy Palermo. She protected herself. She knew she could trust her business partners. But this felt different.

The other woman set down the bowl in her hands and smiled. "Lucy, it's been a long time."

Marsha's husband, Chuck, had been an elder in her father's church. They'd been real converts, always backing up the scripture that Lucy's dad taught.

"It has been a long time," Lucy concurred. "How are you?"

Marsha gave her a look of sympathy, which was almost more than Lucy could handle.

"Chuck left," Marsha told her. "Actually, I helped him out of the house with his suitcase."

"I'm glad you're okay," Lucy told her. And she meant it.

Dane's fingers touched hers. It was gentle but sweet.

Maybe a bit brave on his part. And she appreciated the gesture. At sixteen she'd felt safe with him. She'd never allowed another man to touch her heart or emotions the way he had.

She never wanted to feel that loss again. She took a deep breath and stepped away. "We should get busy."

Pastor Matthews nodded his head, indicated they should follow. "I have everything in my office, including diagrams for placing the system."

"I'd prefer to look things over and make my own diagram," Lucy informed him. She was ready to work on something that would engage her mind and keep her from thoughts that would only lead to trouble.

"What do you need?" the pastor asked as they walked through the door of his office.

"I'll look at doors, windows, any point of entrance. We'll need the best place for the keypad."

She could hear women talking. She followed the sound to where the group sat together in a small living room. There were five women, with Bibles open. They looked up when she entered. Two quickly looked away, but not before she saw bruises.

It brought back memories—this place, the lost expressions, the bruises. As she stepped back into the office she ignored Dane.

"If you'll give me a tour, I'll start taking notes and diagramming placement. Dane can take whatever notes he needs for the electrical aspect of the system."

The phone rang. Pastor Matthews gave them an apologetic look. "I have to get this."

"I can walk her through it," Dane offered.

The pastor was already reaching for his phone. Lucy headed for the door with Dane close behind. As she headed down the hall he caught up to her, tall, powerful, confident. Together they stepped outside, into bright sunlight.

It slayed her that with him close she felt a shift in who she was and what she'd believed about herself since she'd joined the Army at eighteen.

"I saw a Realtor pulling in your driveway this morning." She said the first thing that came to mind, because equal footing was needed.

He gave her a long, careful look, his blue eyes searching hers. She wondered if he would make something up or tell the truth. She knew how to read body language, and his stance said he was being cautious.

Good for him.

"Did you?" he asked. It wasn't really a question.

"I would have him take the signs off the doors if you don't want everyone in town to know." She changed the subject, for his sake, and proceeded to walk around the exterior of the building. Dane followed close behind.

"I worry about Issy," he said finally. She had stopped walking and was studying a window, wondering if there was any part of this building that didn't pose a threat.

"I think that's only natural."

"The school here is good. But I'm not sure if they'll have a program or teachers for her."

"I think by law they have to provide whatever resources are necessary."

He took the end of the tape measure she held out for him.

"That's what I've been told. But I want her to have more opportunities." He narrowed the distance between them and his eyes, blue like a late summer day, held her attention. "I would appreciate it if you didn't tell anyone."

"I'm not going to tell anyone. But tell your real estate agent to be more discreet."

"I will. Thanks."

He was planning to move. She told herself it didn't matter. She hadn't come home with any real plans for staying. Not indefinitely. Not in Bluebonnet.

So why did the idea of Dane and Issy leaving town bother her so much?

For the next half hour Dane followed Lucy as she took notes, made diagrams and talked to herself about the lack of security. This version of Lucy was more interesting than the girl he'd once known. She had layers. She was self-contained but loyal. She tried to keep herself separate from others but she couldn't help but get involved.

Was it just a dozen years ago that he'd been convinced he would marry Lucy Palermo? At the time he'd wanted nothing more than to take her away from here. He'd wanted to rescue her from her father. He'd wanted to protect her.

After a while he'd chalked those emotions up to being a teenager with a hero complex. His parents, aware that he'd been secretly dating her, had explained that he was too young and inexperienced to handle someone who had been through everything Lucy had gone through. Wanting to rescue someone wasn't the same as loving them. And in the end, she'd rescued herself by leaving town.

He thought back to the summer day when he'd met her at the back fence of the Palermo ranch. They'd brought a picnic lunch, and then they'd lain flat on their backs to stare up at the summer sky. The grass had been warm and smelled of sweet clover and dry earth. Their hands had touched, just the tips of their fingers making a connection that had seemed sweet.

"We should finish. I have to get lunch for Maria."

Her words drew him back to the present. "Right."

She walked through the common area, where a few women were sitting, the television on a morning news and entertainment program. She paused, just briefly, as one of the women mentioned that just once when her husband came at her, she wished she could give him a taste of what he'd been giving her.

Lucy kept walking. She knocked on Pastor Matthews's office door, then entered when he called out that the door was open.

"You need to teach these women to defend themselves," she said as she dropped her notes on his desk.

Pastor Matthews looked at her, then his gaze connected with Dane's. Dane shrugged. He was only too happy to help the ministry. He'd give his time and expertise. But going head-to-head with Lucy was not on his list of things he wanted to do.

When she wanted something, he doubted seriously if she would back down. If she felt something was important, she was probably going to keep at it until she accomplished her goal. She was a survivor.

"I'm not sure about that," Pastor Matthews began.

"Why not?" Lucy asked, taking a seat in the office. "I'm not encouraging fighting. I want to give them tools to protect themselves."

"I'll definitely consider it."

"I'm willing to teach them," Lucy offered. She glanced at her watch. "I have to get to Essie's. But I'll be back to install the system now that we have it planned out."

"I'm heading to Essie's myself, I'll meet you there," Dane chimed in.

What was he thinking? He'd practically invited her to lunch, which was the last thing he should be doing. Lucy stared at him as if he'd grown another head. And the good pastor wore an altogether too-amused look.

Fortunately Lucy didn't answer. She shook her head, mumbled something about his sanity and walked out the door. He followed at a distance because it seemed a bit safer.

When they reached the parking lot, she got in her truck, started it and drove away. Dane laughed as he followed her. She'd made it obvious she wasn't interested. He knew better than to pursue this. And yet, he was heading toward Essie's with a determination he hadn't felt in years.

If he had any sense at all, he'd drive on back to the ranch. He'd eat a bologna sandwich with Miss Lois and Issy. He'd make sure the mare with colic was still on the road to recovery because he didn't want to lose her. Not only because of her value but because she had a sweet disposition and in time she'd make a good child's horse.

Maybe he'd let Issy ride her. Someday.

Not that he really wanted to face that day. He knew he would have to let his daughter have her independence. He knew she'd have to go places without him. Someday she would date. Someday she would leave home. He kept telling himself he had time. And right now he wanted to keep her safe. Protect her.

His mom often told him it wasn't bad to be a protector, as long as he understood that people didn't always need protecting. Sometimes protection felt like suffocation.

He thought about Lucy's plan to teach the women

self-defense. He got it. Self-defense was a step toward independence for them.

It would make them feel strong.

When had Lucy learned to protect herself?

Pulling up to Essie's café, he parked his truck next to Lucy's. She shot him a glowering look, the heat of it could be felt through both truck windows. She didn't appreciate him being here. Rather than backing down, he winked at her and got out of his truck. She was already on the sidewalk but he noticed she didn't stomp away, mad. Instead she slowed her steps, waiting for him.

"I'm not sure why you're doing this," she said quietly.

"Because a long time ago we were friends."

She paused midstride. "Friends?"

Okay, they weren't really friends. But they shared things friends would have shared. They told each other secrets. She'd told him things that he'd promised never to tell a soul. He wondered if anyone else knew those things about her.

"I'm not that girl anymore, Dane. We're two completely different people. You have a daughter and you are a part of this community and this church. I avoid everything that has to do with church."

He wanted to tell her she was more involved than she would admit. But she might run off, leaving Maria to her own devices.

He chose safer words. "We're all different people, Lucy. Life does that to us. We learn things about ourselves and about other people, some of it good, some bad."

He'd planned to be married forever. When he'd met Tamara in college he'd known they had nothing in common but he'd loved her, and he'd hoped—prayed—they would overcome the differences. He'd wanted a family, the ranch, church on Sundays. She'd wanted an apartment in the city, Sundays in bed and no children.

"You're still following me," she accused with a hint of humor in her voice.

"No, I'm walking next to you. There's a subtle difference."

A snuffle and oink behind them interrupted the conversation. He pulled Lucy to the edge of the sidewalk as the brown, potbellied pig ambled past, snuffling a bit at their legs before continuing on his journey.

"What was that?" She pulled her arm free from his hand.

"That would be Gatsby." He reached for the door to Essie's.

"Seriously, you're going to tell me a pig named Gatsby just walked down the sidewalk, and then you're going to act as if nothing happened?"

"Gatsby belongs to Homer Wilkins. Unfortunately Homer's fence isn't the best. Or maybe Gatsby is the greatest escape artist ever. Either way, the pig likes to take a stroll from time to time. He pilfers in gardens, digs up yards, and then he goes home. Or someone gathers him up and takes him home."

"This doesn't happen in Austin."

"See what you're missing out on living in the city," he teased.

"See what *you'll* be missing out on," she said.

"Touché."

"You might want to think about that, Dane. You love this town. Your daughter is loved here. Do you really want to take her away from this? For what? A better school?"

"Better opportunities," he reminded her.

"Right, better opportunities."

But her quietly spoken words fueled his indecision. Two weeks ago he'd thought he'd known exactly what he needed to do. Two weeks ago he'd thought he had everything planned.

He hadn't considered that plans could change in an instant. Because of a woman with haunted eyes and a hesitant smile.

The words from moments ago took a crazy twist in his mind. Because standing in front of him was a woman that made him think about everything he'd been missing out on.

Chapter Seven

Dane woke up early Friday morning. A little hand patted his face. Then a little voice whispered something about pancakes. He cracked open one eye and squinted at the barely there light shining through the blinds. His daughter's internal clock didn't always work the way it should. Sometimes he hoped for more than five hours of sleep a night.

"Too early, Issy."

She rested her head on his shoulder, then squirmed her way onto the bed to sit on the edge, feet dangling over the side. "I had a bad dream."

"Did you?" He lifted his arm and cuddled her close.

She nodded. "I dreamed I ate pickles. And a bug."

"That is a bad dream. Do you think you can go back to sleep?"

She shook her head.

"Okay, pancakes it is."

The life of a single dad. He smiled as he carried her down the hall a few minutes later. She was half-asleep, her head on his shoulder. The burst of energy that had woken her at five in the morning seemed to be short-lived.

"Want to lie on the couch while I cook?"

She nodded but her arms remained tight around his neck.

"Don't let go, Daddy," she said in a quiet, sleepy voice.

He sat down, holding her tight, rocking in the recliner just enough to keep her sleeping.

"Sing," she whispered.

One foot on the floor, the other crossed over his knee, he kept the motion of the chair going while he sang about buying her a mockingbird. And if that mockingbird didn't sing, he would buy her a diamond ring. His voice sounded too loud in the quiet of early morning, even though he did his best to sing quietly.

Issy didn't seem to mind. Before long her little body felt heavy against him and her breathing slowed. He kept up the rocking motion, unwilling to get up or let go. He knew it would come, that day in the future when he would have to let go. He knew he would never stop protecting her. But he would have to let go.

For some reason his thoughts shifted to Lucy Palermo. It seemed dangerous in the stillness of early morning to have her on his mind. He shook his head to clear the thoughts away.

"Someone wake up early?"

The whisper didn't startle him. Haven almost always got up early. Either she would have a morning shift at the hospital or she would saddle her mare and go for a long ride. This morning she was dressed for riding. Her hair, curly like Issy's, was pulled back with a headband. Her jeans were tucked into riding boots.

"She thought it was breakfast time. She fell back to sleep before we could make pancakes."

Haven sat on the edge of the sofa, toying with her

headband for a minute before giving him a long, careful look.

"You looked pretty ferocious when I came in. Everything okay?" his sister asked.

"It's good. I was just thinking." He didn't want to admit that his thoughts had taken him down a dead end path, straight to Lucy.

"About the ranch?"

"Among other things." He couldn't remember a time the two of them hadn't shared. He knew her secrets. She knew that he didn't hide much. Right now, he didn't feel like sharing. He didn't know how to explain that Lucy's return had taken him by surprise.

"The people who came by yesterday seemed pretty interested."

His daughter shifted in his arms but her eyes remained closed. "Are you having second thoughts?"

She shrugged. They were partners in the ranch, although nursing was her real love. She loved helping people. And he could tell from the look in her eyes that she had zeroed in on him as if he was the one in need of healing.

"We don't have to sell," he told her. "We have a good foreman and good ranch hands. I could rent a place in Austin."

"What do *you* want?" Haven asked. "Because if you're not happy, she won't be happy, either."

The question stirred some unexpected thoughts in his mind. When he looked up, his sister pinned him with a knowing gaze. Well, that was unfortunate.

"I'm praying, Haven. That's all I can do for now. This ranch is part of our heritage and it's in our blood. But when I think about the future, I think about what I can give my daughter that will make her life easier."

"I know you're torn. I'm sorry." She gave him a quick hug. "I'm going riding. I won't make this any harder on you, but I am going to point something out. I don't think you had any second thoughts about selling until Lucy Palermo came back into town."

"Thanks for pointing that out. You're not turning matchmaker on me, are you?"

"Not at all. I'm never getting married. Why should I push the institution on my brother?"

"Remember, I already gave marriage a go and it wasn't a success."

"That wasn't your fault."

"Said like a truly loyal sibling." He would have walked away from the conversation but for the sleeping little girl in his arms. His sister, when she had something on her mind, could be like a dog with a bone. She wasn't going to give up. He wasn't going to escape.

"Have you talked to Mom and Dad lately?"

Their parents were always a good way to change subjects. She wagged her finger at him.

"Yes, and nice try. I'm going up to Dallas to see them this weekend. I'll probably stay several days. If Lois can't watch Issy, maybe Maria can help out?"

"Yes, she's willing to watch her anytime. She's good with her."

"Maria?"

"Yes, Maria."

Haven chuckled. "Just remember, all work and no play makes my brother old before his time."

He could say the same about his sister but he knew her heartache. He hadn't suffered the same pain. He hadn't been broken the way she'd been broken. That she was whole today, or mostly whole, was a tribute to her faith and her strength.

"I'm happy," he told her. "I have Issy and the ranch. That's all I need right now."

For the past couple of years it had been plenty. He'd been content. He'd always told himself that if he lost that contentment he would consider changes.

"Yes, that's all you need." Haven appeared to agree. "Until it isn't." She left him sitting, giving a salute as she headed outside.

There were very specific reasons he wouldn't date. His marriage to Tamara had taught him two things. Don't marry a woman who isn't interested in staying. And don't marry a woman who doesn't share your faith.

Lucy had good reasons for avoiding church. What she didn't get was that faith had nothing in common with the type of religion her dad had preached.

Not that it mattered.

He had everything he needed. Except, maybe he didn't. He thought about the time spent with Lucy, sharing their concerns with one another, working together. Maybe he did want to find a woman he could share his life with.

A woman who would be a partner in life.

Lucy had been working on the installation of the security system for an hour. For the first fifteen minutes she'd been alone. But then she'd become aware of her audience, a boy of about five. He had hidden behind the door and she'd caught him peeking out at her. He wasn't very good at sneaking.

Now, forty-five minutes into his surveillance, she decided he should come out of hiding.

"I need someone to hold my tools if you'd like to help."

He reminded her of children she'd met in Afghanistan. They'd witnessed and experienced abuse, different than this child, but still it had changed them. She'd used American candy to befriend those Afghan children. The ones who had hidden in doorways, behind walls, in the shadows. Eventually they had ventured out. Chocolate was a universal language.

The memories were bittersweet. Some of those children were still alive in Afghanistan. Some had been lost in the mire of war. Others had joined groups that fought against the American soldiers. One of those children had led Lucy and her friends into a trap.

"What are the wires for?" the little guy at her side asked as he took the screwdriver from her hand, and then the hammer.

"To keep you safe," she answered. Children needed truthful answers, but not ones that would frighten them or keep them awake at night.

"From my daddy?" he asked.

She looked down at him, at blond hair and big gray eyes. He had a bruise on his cheek. She should have noticed sooner. She should do something to make him feel safe. He made the decision for her. He moved close to her side, sliding beneath her arm. She wrapped him in her arms and wanted to promise his daddy would never hurt him again.

She couldn't make that promise.

"Yes, the wires will keep you safe." She hoped.

"Can I help?" he asked.

"Yes, you can." She started a screw, and then showed him how to place the screwdriver. "Can you do that for me?"

He nodded, his bottom lip caught between his teeth.

Soon she felt someone else had joined them. She knew he stood just to the right of the door. She glanced back over her shoulder and caught him watching, the brim of his white cowboy hat pulled low. He moved just inside and leaned a shoulder against the door frame.

She gave her full attention to the little boy at her side, making sure that the wires would keep him safe from his daddy.

"What's your name?" she asked.

"Tyler," he answered, still concentrating hard on the screw.

"How old are you?"

"Five. I start kindergarten soon."

"You're going to like school." She put her hand over his to help him with the screwdriver.

"I like Sunday school." He looked up at her with trusting gray eyes. "Do you?"

She was aware that Dane had walked farther into the room. He was watching, listening. Tyler had asked her a question.

Mrs. Gordon. Sweetest Sunday school teacher Lucy had ever had. She'd read them Bible stories and let them move felt figures on the board.

"Yes, I like Sunday school."

"Can I help you two?" Dane stood behind them now.

Tyler suddenly tensed up. Of course he did. She gave him an encouraging hug and started him working on another screw, one she didn't really need, but he seemed to want to do something positive.

"Of course you can help." She'd been kneeling with Tyler for longer than she'd realized. Long enough that her knees were stiff and she didn't mind that Dane offered her a hand to pull her to her feet.

"How much have you gotten done? I planned to be here earlier but Issy slept late after a restless night. I took her to Maria and brought pancakes for both of them."

"Thank you for feeding Maria and the tadpole." She glanced down at the little boy now standing next to her. She ruffled a hand through his soft blond hair. "We haven't done much. But we'll need some wiring done. I'm sticking to the plan we made the other day."

"Gotcha. I'll get started on that. I noticed the women were in the kitchen. Pastor Matthews told me to pass on the message that we're invited to lunch."

Invited to lunch. She wanted to reject the invitation. She had things to do at the ranch. Her brother Alex had called and he was planning to come home. He thought that together they could get things back in shape, maybe replace the cattle that had been sold off and buy a few horses. She hadn't told him yet that she had no intention of staying in Bluebonnet and being a rancher.

"Tyler and I are going to get a little more done on this, and then we'll head to the kitchen."

Dane stood there, watching her, probably trying to figure her out.

"I'll take a look at the wiring and when you're ready for lunch, let me know and I'll walk down with you."

The man didn't give up easily. She remembered that about him. She remembered the day after her dad had caught them together. He'd demanded her father tell him where she was.

She thought he probably still didn't know where her dad had hidden her. She couldn't imagine ever telling him. There were some things too painful to share, too painful to think about.

Tyler tugged on her shirttail. "I'm hungry."

Lucy glanced around the room, at the work still needing to be done. And then she looked at the little boy, his gray eyes imploring her.

"Guess it's lunchtime."

Dane had been almost at the door. "I'll just head that way with you."

Tyler ran ahead of them, leaving Lucy alone with Dane.

"Do people know you're a softy?" he asked.

"No, they don't. So don't tell."

"Never," he teased. "But I'm not surprised."

"Aren't you?" She glanced up at him, getting lost for a moment in the blue of his eyes.

"Not at all. You were always watching over someone. Kids at school who were being bullied, your little sister, even those rotten brothers of yours."

"The curse of the older sibling. You do the same with Haven."

"Maybe."

The women in the kitchen were talking and laughing. Tyler was sitting on the counter eating a slice of corn bread. Someone mentioned Gatsby the pig. He had been seen at the church and one of the kids had tried to catch him.

She'd never felt really attached to this church or this town, not even to the people here, but seeing both through the eyes of an adult changed things. Maybe time and distance had helped her sort out all her feelings, toward her father and the town.

As an adult she could see that God and her father's church were not one and the same. The town, although they hadn't done a lot to help, had done small things to ease the way. It had been one of the neighboring farmers who had given her a lift to Austin on the day she left home.

He'd asked if she was sure. She'd told him she was eighteen and she was joining the Army. He'd wished her the best and dropped her off at the recruiting station. For the next month she'd worked hard, staying at a cheap hotel until she could leave for Basic Training.

A hand touched her back. She felt the warmth of Dane at her side and she told herself to move away. Getting attached to him was mistake number one. She knew better. Staying detached meant staying safe.

"Are you two joining us for lunch?" Pastor Matthews asked as he breezed into the room. She wondered if the man ever had a bad day.

"I know I am." Dane had moved away, his hand sliding off her back. He took a bowl one of the women handed him and he passed it to Lucy.

She accepted, but then her phone rang. She set the bowl down to answer.

"Maria?" she answered. "Is everything okay?"

Dane was instantly on alert. Of course he was; his daughter was with her sister.

"I'm sick." Maria's voice was weak. "I'm trying to keep Issy with me, but I'm afraid I can't watch her the way I should."

"I'll be home in five minutes. Sit in the bathroom with Issy, and I'll come get her."

Dane didn't give her a chance to explain. He was heading for the door and she caught up with him.

"Hey, she's fine," she called out to his retreating back.

He hesitated, just long enough for her to catch up. "It didn't sound as if everything was fine."

"Issy is okay. Maria is sick. I'll run out there, right the ship and you do whatever you need to do in town."

He looked torn and she wondered how often he

trusted his little girl with others. He trusted Maria, Lois and Haven. But did he let anyone else help?

"I can do this," she assured him.

He took off his hat and swiped a hand through his short, dark hair. "Yeah, I know. And I should have realized this was too much for Maria. She needs to take care of herself right now."

"I know she does." Lucy hadn't realized, though. She hadn't thought about Maria being pregnant, sick, watching a little girl. "I'll go home and make sure they're fine."

"You need to make her a doctor's appointment."

"Right. I think she has one coming up. Doc Parker did the initial exam but he told her she has to go to an obstetrician."

"I'm going to finish up what I can here, run by the feed store and then I'll be out to get Issy. But if, for whatever reason, you need me to come home sooner, I can."

As she left she realized something about being home. She did have friends. She'd trusted her business partners, Boone and Daron, to have her back. They'd trusted her the same way. But her circle of friends had been small.

Coming home to Bluebonnet, the circle had grown. And it included more than family. It included neighbors. And a man who was definitely more than a friend.

Chapter Eight

Lucy and Issy were playing in the yard with one of the kittens when Dane showed up to get his daughter. He asked about Maria, who had gone to bed as soon as Lucy got home, then he loaded up his daughter and drove away. Lucy was still standing on the front porch when a truck and trailer came down the driveway, the dust of Dane's truck still circling.

She headed for the stable, the direction the newly arrived truck and trailer were heading. When she got there, her brother Alex was out and the back of the trailer was open.

"Welcome home," he said as he unloaded a mare from the trailer. She was a deep red and fidgety. As she stood in the yard, ears attentive, Lucy stepped forward to admire her.

"I could say the same to you," Lucy said as she looked the animal over.

He grinned, managing to look far younger than his twenty-five years. "Yeah, I guess you could. How's Maria?"

"Sick. I'd take her to the doctor but I'm not sure they

can do much for morning sickness. Or in her case, all-day sickness."

"Probably not." He handed her the lead rope. "Early Christmas gift. Hold her and I'll unload her best friend."

He returned a minute later with a dusky gray pony. The smaller animal surveyed his surroundings, ears flicking and dark eyes curious.

She reached to pet the sleek, red neck of the mare. The horse turned, nuzzling at her shoulder. "Her best friend is a pony?"

Alex flashed a dimpled grin. "Yeah. I couldn't leave her behind. I figure Maria's little one will be able to ride her someday."

From behind Lucy came an excited screech.

"Alex, she's perfect. And you're home." Maria hurried to join them and she immediately made a beeline to her brother, gave him a hug and then turned her attention to the pony.

Lucy gave her little sister a suspicious look. "I thought you were sick. Now you're all dressed up. At three in the afternoon?"

"I'm going to church. I thought I told you."

Lucy felt her heart shudder. "No. You didn't tell me."

Maria gave her a sheepish grin. "Sorry. It's an afternoon Bible study, not regular church. I told Bessy that maybe we could give her a ride. Because her car won't start and Nina Tucker usually gives her a ride. But Nina is in the hospital."

Nina and Bessy. They had gone to Jesse Palermo's church. Not for long. Both had been too knowledgeable of the Bible and unwilling to bend to her father's will.

Maria's words sank in. "You told Bessy I would give her a ride to church? Me?"

"Just a ride, Luce. You don't have to go in."

Lucy led the horse to a stall. Maria and Alex followed. He put the pony in a stall next to the mare as their little sister leaned over the stall door to shower the little gray with love and attention.

"She'll be a good pony for your little girl," Alex said, switching the conversation to something neutral.

"Or boy," Lucy argued, thankful for the reprieve he'd bought her.

"We'll know soon enough." Maria continued to pet the pony. "But I don't really care. Boy or a girl, the baby will be a blessing. So about church?"

"I'll drive you to church, Maria. But I'm not going to the Bible study."

"I understand."

"What time do we need to leave?" Lucy asked.

"In about an hour. And can we pick up Bessy Moore, too?" Maria asked with a hopeful grin. "You don't have to go in if you don't want. Just drop us off and I'll text when we're finished."

"That sounds good. I'm going to throw something together for dinner. Alex, you eating with us?"

Alex glanced at her from the mare's stall, nodding as he did. "Yeah. But I'm with you. I'm not going to church."

When they reached the church, Lucy helped Bessy out of the truck. The older woman, with her gray hair styled in a neat bun, smiled up at Lucy. Bessy wore a pretty print dress, white gloves and orthopedic shoes. She hadn't changed much since Lucy had left home.

"You're sure you won't come in with us?"

Lucy shook her head. "No, but I'll be out here waiting to give you a ride home."

"It isn't the same," Bessy said quietly, her gloved hand on Lucy's arm.

"I know it isn't." It was hard to admit it. But she knew the people in this building weren't the same as the ones who had been there when her father held control of his small flock.

Church wasn't the enemy. God wasn't the controlling figure her father had made him out to be. She'd known wonderful, loving Christians since she'd left Bluebonnet. She realized, as an adult, that she'd known plenty of good people in this town who hadn't gone to her dad's church.

"Someday?" Bessy asked, her smile sweet.

Lucy found she couldn't resist Bessy. Her heart softened a bit as she looked at the older woman. "Someday."

Bessy and Maria left together, Maria holding the arm of the older woman, helping her over rough ground. Lucy stood next to her truck for a long time, watching as people parked and went inside. She could hear the voices raised in song. The old piano rattled the windows. It seemed a bit more than an ordinary Bible study.

Lucy walked around the building. From inside she could hear Pastor Matthews but his words were muffled. The congregation laughed at whatever he'd said. There was silence for a moment. She walked on, toward the back door.

She entered the building and walked down the hallway to the nursery, a small room with bright walls painted with Bible scenes. Noah's ark on one wall, Jesus with children on the other. The walls were the same. That surprised her. It haunted her. She stood in the doorway. Children in the room looked up from their play to watch the stranger in their midst. The woman sitting in a rocking chair pushed herself to her feet.

"Lucy?" The nursery worker spoke quietly, smiling down at the children as she moved toward the door. "It's me, Opal Lawrence. We were in school together."

Lucy took a deep breath and remembered.

"Yes, of course."

Relief came over Opal's face. "You can come in if you'd like."

Lucy watched the children play. Issy was there. She had turned toward the door, a doll in her arms. "Lucy?"

The little girl stood and took a few hesitant steps.

Lucy stepped into the room. "Hey, Issy."

"Is my daddy here?" Issy eased forward. Lucy took hold of her hand.

"No, just me. Do you want me to read to you?"

Issy nodded so Lucy led her to a chair. The two of them sat together. Opal handed Lucy a book about David and Goliath. She opened it and found it was a pop-up story. She guided Issy's hands to the figures of David, his sheep, and then the giant, Goliath. She read the story and with each page the little girl felt the characters.

As Lucy read, the other children gathered close, standing at her side, near her feet or even sitting on the floor. She told of the five stones and the slingshot, and one little girl reminded her that David's faith killed the giant, because that rock was little and giants are taller than the ceiling.

When Lucy finished the story, she looked up and realized she had an audience. Dane stood there, in dark jeans and a button-up shirt with the sleeves rolled to his elbows. He was leaning against the door frame, his arms crossed over his chest. His blue eyes were serious but the corners of his mouth turned up a bit, enough to know he wasn't upset. He pushed away from the door and she felt small in the chair, his daughter on her lap. He was tall, and yet moved with the lithe power of a rancher, a cowboy.

"Lucy," he greeted her, his voice soft. "Issy, did you like the story?"

Leaning against Lucy, Dane's daughter smiled and nodded her head. "It was about giants. And giants are big," Issy told him. She stuck a thumb in her mouth and her other hand opened the book to touch the pop-ups.

Dane squatted next to her chair, reaching to smooth Issy's hair as he did. His hand brushed Lucy's shoulder and she didn't pull away.

His touch felt complicated.

And she'd never been one for complications. Never. And yet, here she sat with Dane's daughter on her lap.

"I didn't expect to see you here," Dane said as he stood. His hands were clasped behind his back.

"I gave Maria a ride to town. Were you at the study?"

"No. I had a meeting with a few of the board members concerning some changes we need to make."

Issy wiggled from her lap and took hold of Dane's hand. Something happened in that moment as she watched the little girl and her father. She made a decision that complicated her life. Intentionally. Without remorse. "I have a roast in the slow cooker if you and Issy would like to join us."

"An invitation to dinner? And you cooked?"

"Don't expect too much. This is a first for me."

He took his daughter in his arms. "We would love to join you."

As he left she sat there wondering what had come

over her. She didn't like complications. She never complicated her life. And yet, she'd just invited two of them to her home.

The house smelled good, the way a house with dinner in the slow cooker should smell. Dane led Issy by the hand, following Maria to the kitchen. He could hear Lucy talking to someone and she didn't sound happy. Maybe they had unexpected company. Could be her brother Alex.

Maria glanced back at him, an apologetic look on her face.

"I promise you, she doesn't always talk to our food," the younger woman explained.

"Are you sure she's talking to the food? She sounds mad."

"Alex went to town and no one else is here."

They entered the kitchen and sure enough, Lucy was standing over the slow cooker, a fork in one hand and a cookbook in the other. She frowned at the meat in the cooker and jabbed at it again.

"This is not the way you're supposed to look. Falling off the bone, the recipe says. Juicy and tender, it says."

"Problem?" Dane lifted Issy in his arms and approached Lucy carefully, because an angry woman wielding a fork couldn't be a good thing.

She glared at him and went back to reading the cookbook. "It said four hours on high. It's been cooking for four hours. It's still pink. And the vegetables are brown."

He took the fork and prodded the meat, leaning in next to her. "Did you thaw it before you put it in here?"

"The recipe doesn't say thaw before cooking. If it

takes something four hours to cook, I'm assuming it's frozen and that's why it takes so long."

"It's a *slow cooker*, Luce." Maria giggled. Then she took a few quick steps out of the danger zone.

"Well, if the meat needs to be thawed, they should say that in the directions." Lucy's cheeks turned a little pink. "We'll have ham sandwiches instead."

"We can fix this." Dane looked around the kitchen. "Do you have a baking sheet? And foil?"

"Yes and yes," Maria answered. She was already digging in the cabinets. The foil landed on the counter, then a baking sheet. "There you go. What are you going to do with it?"

"Throw it on the grill." Dane had glanced out the window and spotted a gas grill. "As long as you have gas in that tank."

"You don't have to do this," Lucy told him. "I invited you for dinner. I didn't invite you over to cook."

"No, but I'm here. We have to eat and I'm decent with a grill. I think the vegetables will have to be sacrificed. We can just heat up a can of green beans. Let's look and see what you have in the cabinets."

Issy was clinging to his leg. He reached to pick her up again and turned to Maria, who stood nearby. "Maria, could you hang out with Issy for a few minutes?"

The teenager took his daughter almost too willingly. There was a definite mischievous glint in her brown eyes. When she glanced from him to Lucy, he nearly took Issy back.

But Issy willingly left with Maria. The two went out the back door, the poodle following along behind them. That left him alone with Lucy in the kitchen. She stood there fidgeting. Another surprise, her fidgeting. She watched him, shifting from foot to foot, drawing his attention. Then he noticed her feet were bare and her toenails were painted pink.

He had to fight hard to hide his amusement.

"So what do we do now?" she asked.

"We'll start by getting this roast out of the cooker. By the way, did you make Maria a doctor's appointment?"

"I did. It's Monday."

He started working and she moved in to his side to watch. She was close, her shoulder brushing his and those painted toenails distracting him. He cleared his throat and focused on the task at hand, the roast. Not Lucy Palermo, standing so close he caught a hint of something floral and feminine. It matched the toenails, not the woman he knew.

It reminded him of the girl, carefree and a little wild when no one was looking. Back then she'd laughed a little, with the windows down on his truck and the radio blasting. He'd pulled to the side of the road and kissed her.

He cleared his throat and she looked up at him. Did she not remember? Or did she choose to block memories that had turned dark the day her dad caught up with them at the swimming hole, a place she wasn't allowed to go?

"I could go with you all." In for a penny, in for a pound. It was a mistake. He knew it but he couldn't back out now.

"I don't know," she answered with better sense than he seemed to have at that moment. "Let's just focus on dinner and the roast."

"Right, dinner." He used tongs to pull the roast out of the slow cooker.

Laughter rang out from the backyard, where Issy played with Maria. He glanced out the window and watched as the two walked with the dog following, Issy's hand in Maria's. Lucy came over to look out the window.

"Good thing you're here. We would have been eating ham sandwiches and the dog would have had roast." As she joked with him, she flashed him one of her rare smiles and it eased the tension inside him.

"I think thirty minutes and it'll be done."

He picked up the tray and headed for the back door. Lucy started to follow but the doorbell rang.

"I can get this started by myself," he told her.

He got the grill going, and then he sat back to watch Issy and Maria. They were sitting just feet away from each another. Maria had found a ball and she rolled it to his daughter, who sat on the ground with her legs out. Issy would laugh as it hit her hands and she would push it back to the teenager.

For several minutes he watched, in awe that the laughing little girl was his. He should have thought about playing ball with her. He guessed there were a lot of things he should have thought of, ways to help her. As much as he wanted to protect her, he also wanted her to be independent.

A hand touched his shoulder. Without thinking, he covered it with his own. Lucy's skin was soft beneath his. Her hands, though she seemed strong, were fine boned, graceful.

"She's happy," Lucy said.

"Yes, she is. I…" What was he going to say? "I hope I'm doing the right thing."

Selling the ranch. Moving away from Bluebonnet. A few weeks ago it had seemed like the perfect plan. She looked at him.

"You are. But just because it's right, doesn't mean it's easy."

She said it in such a way that he knew she'd made choices that weren't always easy, but she felt they were right. He wondered if she included coming home in the category of "right but not easy."

"Who was at the front door?" he asked. She pulled her hand away from his.

"Aunt Essie. Alex stopped by to see her and told her I'd put a roast in the slow cooker. For some reason she thought that warranted a visit. She's getting potato salad out of her truck."

Issy, tired of playing ball, walked his way. She had hold of Maria's hand and she took careful steps as Maria coached her over tough spots in the terrain. She grabbed her up when she got to the patio and said something funny, making his daughter giggle. Everyone smiled when Issy laughed.

"I have something to show you," Lucy said, the words coming sudden and unsure.

"Something to show me?" He stood and lowered the temperature on the grill. "Right now?"

"No, not now. Later." She hesitated. "It's not a big deal."

Essie stepped out the back door, glancing between the two of them. "Why not now? I'll watch the meat. You all go and see what it is that has Lucy on hot coals."

Lucy shot her aunt a warning look. "I'm not on hot coals."

Essie shrugged it off and gave her full attention to their meal. "Suit yourself, Luce."

"Really, it can wait."

Curiosity got the best of him. "Maybe I can't wait."

He picked up his daughter, shifting her to his left side and reaching for Lucy with his free right hand.

They stood for several long seconds like that and finally she nodded.

"Let's go."

She led them out a side gate and then to the stable. As they walked, Dane noticed the changes that were taking place on the Palermo ranch. Cleaner fencerows, a barn that looked as if someone had finally taken an interest. There were more cattle grazing out in the field.

When they got to the stable, Dane reached to open the door. He held it as she walked in, flipping on lights as she went. He noticed the room next to the tack room had been boarded up. It was recent, the boards were new.

"You don't want to use that room?" he asked her.

"No. I don't."

"What if you…"

She spun to face him. "I will *never* need to go in there."

Her expression froze him. Before he could even process what she'd said, she walked away.

A pretty chestnut stuck her head over the stall door. Lucy stopped to stroke the animal's face. She leaned close to the horse, her back to him for a long moment, then with a deep breath she moved on.

"Nice horse." Dane stopped to look the mare over.

"Alex brought her with him."

She stopped in front of the next stall. This time a head didn't reach over the stall door, but a tiny nose pushed its way into view.

"Did you buy a large dog?" he teased.

She ignored him. Then she guided Issy's hand to the pony's soft ears, telling his daughter the animal's name was Cobalt. Issy went to Lucy, holding tight with one arm while she petted the pony.

"You bought a pony?"

"Alex brought her. He said she was the mare's best friend so he couldn't leave her behind. We don't have a lot of use for a pony, but he is sweet."

"Maria's baby won't be able to ride for a long time."

"This pony definitely needs a little girl." Lucy looked over his daughter's head, catching his attention with a meaningful look.

He got what she was trying to tell him. His little girl needed a pony. He shook his head, because he wasn't ready for this yet.

"You have to let go sometime," Lucy said softly.

"Easier said than done."

"Yes, I know." She handed Issy to him but his daughter was still reaching for the pony.

He watched as Lucy put a halter and then a lead rope on the pony. The animal didn't fuss. He seemed very happy to have the attention and to be led from the stall. His ears flicked as he took in his surroundings but he didn't shy or move a bit as she dropped the lead rope.

"He won't move until you pick up the lead." Lucy leaned against the stall and smiled at the pony and then at Dane. "Pretty amazing, isn't he?"

He couldn't take his eyes off the woman standing feet away from him. "Yes, amazing."

He looked the animal over, then reached for the lead and sat his daughter on the animal's back, telling her what he planned to do and that she should sit very still.

Issy did exactly as she was told, holding tight to the pony's rounded belly with her tiny legs. She put her hands on the long, silvery-gray mane and leaned just slightly to tell the animal that he was her favorite horse.

"What do you think?" Lucy asked as she came close, her hand going to Issy's back to steady her.

"I love ponies." Issy fairly glowed. Her smile radiated. "Daddy, do you love the pony?"

"I do love the pony," Dane answered.

From a distance he heard Maria calling to them, telling them that dinner was ready. He reached for his daughter as Lucy took the lead rope from his hand. Issy tried to grab hold of the pony.

"I don't want to go, Daddy." She had her hand out, searching for the pony.

"No, we have to go, Isabelle. It's time to eat now." Dane knew what letting go felt like.

Years ago he'd let go of Lucy because he'd known it was best for her, and for him. He'd let go of Tamara. He'd let go of dreams they shared. Letting go of his marriage had taken time. Pastor Matthews had told him to think of it as a death. The death of a marriage, of plans they'd shared and dreams they'd dreamed together. That kind of loss took time to process. It took time to grieve.

He was trying to process the decision he'd made, to let go of the ranch, because that's what it would take to give his daughter a better life.

Lucy put the pony back in his stall and closed the door. Somehow her hand found his and he knew that she understood. She understood letting go. She understood how difficult it was to let another person into your life.

As they neared the house the aroma of meat cooked on the grill wafted through the air. Dane could hear Essie talking to Maria. Alex's truck was parked in front of the house and his voice joined the conversation. The dog began to bark and Maria laughed. Dane, Issy and Lucy walked around the corner of the house, where everyone had gathered in the backyard.

Next to him, Lucy's expression reflected a peace she probably hadn't known growing up. She smiled at Essie, who was busy taking the roast off the grill. Alex was giving her advice. This was family. They'd been broken and beat down, but they were healing. They were able to laugh, to share a meal. He felt a little more whole, just being here with them.

Chapter Nine

Monday morning Dane pulled up to the house and honked. He was driving her and Maria to the ob-gyn appointment in Killeen because he'd told her he had things to get that he couldn't in Bluebonnet. Maria was out the front door before Lucy could lock the dog in the bathroom. She made sure all of the lights were off, the coffeepot was shut off and all the doors were locked.

She took a deep breath, peeked out the window and gave herself a stern lecture about not getting involved with Dane. Then she grabbed her purse and walked out the front door.

"Issy would like for you to play country music," Maria said from the backseat of the truck. "She especially likes Johnny Cash. Don't you, Issy?" Maria leaned close to the little girl and started singing "Folsom Prison Blues."

Issy giggled. "I like Johnny Cash."

Lucy didn't. She'd heard enough Johnny to last a lifetime. Their father had loved Johnny Cash. He'd played it in the barn, in the house and in the car. But it was the barn stereo that haunted her memories. Those familiar songs on repeat. And no escaping them.

Maria wouldn't remember. Dane didn't know. He tossed Maria his phone. "You'll have to find it."

"No Johnny Cash," Lucy said quietly.

"Why, Luce?" Maria asked, even though Johnny was already playing, the volume turned low.

"Please, Maria. Play George. Any George you want. Anything but Johnny."

The music stopped. Maria reached her hand out to touch Lucy's shoulder. "I know it was bad. But we can't do this, where we hide it and pretend it will go away. It isn't healthy. As siblings we should at least talk to each other. Whatever secrets he made you keep, you should talk about because he isn't here to stop you anymore."

"This isn't the time," Lucy warned.

Dane glanced her way but kept driving. He didn't know about Johnny Cash. He wouldn't know because even during those weeks when they'd dated, she'd hidden the truth. She'd wanted a brief, golden moment when everything seemed normal. He'd given her the most normal moments of her teen years.

George Jones came over the speakers. Dane's hand slid across the seat and his fingers touched hers. Lucy felt her cheeks flush.

A short time later they were pulling into the parking lot of the obstetrician's office located in a medical building on the outskirts of Killeen.

From the back Maria made a sound that was almost a sob. Lucy glanced back. Her sister wasn't crying, not really, but her eyes were bright with tears. She looked away, but not before one of those tears rolled down her cheek.

"It's going to be okay," Lucy told her. "We're going to get through this."

Maria nodded, then she cleared her throat. "I keep telling myself that but then reality hits. I'm not even eighteen. I just graduated high school a few months ago. I'm not ready to be a mom. I don't know how I would be a parent every single day."

"It won't be easy."

Maria gave a watery laugh. "You've got that right. And you don't have to lecture me. I lecture myself every day. I knew better. I should have made better choices. It's easy to say those things now, when it's too late to go back. But what do I do about tomorrow?"

"Tomorrow you do your best. Each day you make choices and live with the consequences but you do your best. If I could go back and undo choices I made in the past, I would. But I can't. And so I live with it. But a baby, that's a life. And you'll treasure that life, no matter what."

"I don't want to keep the baby, Luce," Maria whispered.

Dane quietly got out of the truck and removed Issy from her seat. He grabbed Issy's doll and closed the truck door, leaving them alone.

"So what do you plan?" Lucy asked. It came out harsher than she intended.

"Oh, not *that*!" Maria swiped at her face with the palm of her hand, brushing away more tears that escaped. "I'm having the baby. But I meant it when I said I want to give it up for adoption. I want this baby to have two parents. Not a girl just out of high school. Maybe we can find some nice couple and they'll be amazing and she'll be happy. Because I think it's a she. And I want her to be someone's little princess the way Issy is Dane's."

"If you keep her, she'll be a princess."

Maria sighed. "Yes, that's true. I know girls younger than me have babies and they do just fine. But I don't think that's the right choice for me. I want your support in this, Luce."

"You've got it. Whatever you decide, I'm here."

"Here, as in staying in Bluebonnet?"

That took Lucy by surprise.

The silence went on and on, while Maria waited for an answer. Only Lucy didn't know what to say. Maria finally opened the truck door to get out. "Right. I didn't think so."

Lucy caught up with her sister as they crossed the parking lot. "I didn't say I'm not staying. We were talking about choices. I have to make decisions, Maria. I have a business to consider. I never thought that Bluebonnet Springs would be my home or my life. I never dreamed I would want to be back on the ranch."

"I know. You're only here for me. But I don't want to force you to stay. And does it really matter? I'm going to college. I might decide to settle somewhere else. It would just be nice to have you at the house."

"I might have to go away for a few days at a time, but no matter what I'm not going to leave before the baby is born," Lucy assured her little sister.

Maria blew out a sigh. "I'm sorry for doing this to you. Pregnancy makes me cranky. And really, it should be Mom with me."

"But I am here and we'll figure this out," Lucy answered, giving her sister a quick hug.

With nothing settled, they both joined Dane in the lobby of the doctor's office.

While Lucy and Maria filled out some paperwork, Dane sat in a corner of the waiting area. Issy sat next to him talking to her doll. He smiled down at his little girl, her unruly blond curls controlled by a hair band.

His phone rang and he glanced at it. The caller ID showed his real estate agent's number. Dane had to answer, even if he didn't want to. He held the phone up, getting Lucy's attention, and then he pointed to Issy. She nodded and headed their way.

"I've got to take this."

"We'll be fine. If you're not back, we'll take her in with us."

"Thanks," he said as he headed for the door. He answered as he walked out into the heat of early morning. "Jeff, what can I do for you?"

"I've got an offer." The Realtor sounded like a man who knew he was about to make a lot of money.

"Okay."

"You're having second thoughts?"

Dane walked down the sidewalk. "Not really."

But he was having second thoughts. He was having third and fourth thoughts, too. He reminded himself that he was doing this for Issy, then he questioned himself because would she really be better off in Austin, away from the ranch and from people she'd always known?

He didn't want to admit it, even to himself, but he knew that Lucy Palermo had something to do with his second thoughts on the sale. That was a mistake, because he had to make the best decision for Issy.

"Dane, you don't have to do this."

"I know. But I'll listen to the offer."

"That's all I ask. If you don't want to take it, you don't have to. But if you're changing your mind about selling, I need to know that pretty soon because I can't keep showing the property, and then telling buyers it isn't really for sale."

"No, I know you can't. Email me the offer."

"Will do."

Dane walked back inside. Lucy was sitting with Issy. Maria was gone. He sat next to her and his daughter instantly climbed from her lap to his.

"Maria go in?" he asked.

"Yeah. She wanted to do this alone. She says she doesn't want to keep the baby. She wants to find a couple who will adopt it."

"That's a big decision."

Lucy closed her eyes. "Yeah, it is. Sometimes I feel like she's the most mature member of our family. She's been through a lot but she's solid."

"She didn't have to live it the way you and the boys did."

"No, I guess not."

They sat there in silence until he couldn't take it any longer. He had questions. He wanted answers and he knew it wasn't really his business. *She* wasn't his business. But she needed someone to care. She needed to feel like she was more than the person who came to the rescue of her family.

"Johnny Cash?" he asked as Issy curled into his shoulder and dozed.

"Ah, you had to bring that up, didn't you?"

"You don't have to tell me if you really don't want to."

She lifted one shoulder as if it didn't matter. "My

dad's favorite form of punishment. After he caught us together, he locked me in the storage room in the stable."

The boarded-up room. He remained silent, not wanting to stop her from sharing.

"For two days. With Johnny Cash on replay."

His insides tensed and he couldn't say he'd ever felt anger like he felt at that moment. He'd told his parents they needed to go check on her. He'd tried but her dad had turned him away at the front gate to the property. Looking back, he should have done more. But he'd been a kid and the complications of a relationship with Lucy Palermo had been more than he'd been prepared for.

"Don't get that look on your face, Dane. The days of a big rescue attempt are in the past. You couldn't have done anything, not even if you'd tried."

"I should have tried harder, though."

"What would you have done? My dad had people convinced he was decent, a good dad, a family man."

"No one was convinced of that."

She brushed it off. "You couldn't have done anything. And I survived."

"I'm still sorry."

The door to the exam rooms opened, ending the conversation. A nurse stepped out, motioning for Lucy.

"She's having an ultrasound. She wants you back there."

Lucy stood but didn't immediately walk away. She studied him and his daughter, a soft smile easing her expression. She leaned down, placed a hand on his cheek, then she kissed his forehead.

The gesture stunned him.

It was as unexpected as a snowstorm in April and as warm as a breeze off the Gulf Coast.

* * *

Lucy stepped into the darkened room with her sister. Maria was on the exam table looking small, tense and younger than her almost eighteen years. She gave Lucy a tight smile and wiggled fingers in a greeting before clasping her hands over her stomach.

"Have a seat," the technician offered as she typed information into the computer.

Lucy took a seat on the rolling stool next to her sister. She studied the screen as images appeared and then blurred, reappearing again as the technician rolled the ultrasound wand across Maria's belly.

"There's your baby's heart." The technician added an arrow to the picture on the monitor, pointing to the heart beating in the tiny body that rolled and moved inside the bubble on the screen.

Maria clutched Lucy's hand and Lucy used her other hand to dash away the few tears that trickled down her cheeks.

"Look at those ears." The technician grinned back at them.

It took a few minutes. There were more arrows, pointing to fingers, eyes, the baby's nose.

"The baby looks healthy and everything seems to be fine with Mom." The technician hit a button and printed out a few pictures that she handed to Maria. "You'll do great."

Maria studied the pictures of a tiny body. "I'm going to have a baby."

"Yes, you are."

Maria reached for a tissue on a nearby table. "But it's going to be someone else's baby."

"Maria…"

"Just pray about it."

As Maria slid off the table and slid her feet into her shoes, Lucy was thinking of Dane. She wanted to tell him about the baby, about its tiny fingers and big ears.

Chapter Ten

Bluebonnet wasn't crowded when Lucy got there early the next morning. She easily found a parking space on Main Street. She had a prescription to pick up for Maria at the pharmacy. She also needed a few things from the grocery store and she thought she might get lunch at Essie's. Tuesday was chicken and noodles at the café.

As she walked down the sidewalk toward the feed store, Bea Maxwell joined her. The older woman had her hair shoved beneath a hairnet. She wore a floral housedress, knee-high socks and tennis shoes. But Lucy didn't care what Bea wore, the older woman was like walking sunshine.

"Lucy Palermo. Well, land's sakes, girl, you have grown up and gotten prettier than Angus Bradford's best mare. My goodness, that hair of yours shines like silk. Do you use something special on it? I tried using egg whites and mayonnaise on mine but it was hot out and it didn't take too long before that stuff smelled rancid."

That would have been the moment to tell Bea that a concoction like eggs and mayo had to be rinsed out. But before she could, Bea had moved on to her next topic.

"I heard tell your sister, Maria, is in the family way. Jaxon Williams said he isn't going to marry her. And mercy me, I don't think I would want my girl to marry Jaxon. If I had a girl. Which I never did. I haven't even been married. I almost got married once, when I was a young girl. But my mama said I needed to stay home and take care of her like a good girl. So I did. I took care of my mama until she was eighty and losing her mind. She didn't know left from right at the end."

Lucy put a hand on Bea's arm and patted her gently, hoping the older woman would calm down a hair. Bea was simple—that's what folks around Bluebonnet had always said. Lucy would beg to differ. If anyone asked her opinion, she would tell them Bea was just about the most complex woman she'd ever met. Nothing slipped past Bea.

"Bea, are you working at Essie's today?"

The older woman could also cook better than anyone Lucy had ever met. She might be scatterbrained and need someone to keep her on task. But oh, could she cook.

"Oh, yes I am. Are you going to eat lunch at the café? Your aunt said she doesn't know that you'll ever get your head screwed on straight. It's your daddy's fault, apparently."

Lucy bit down on her bottom lip to hide her smile. "Apparently."

"He had chairsisms."

"Charisma?"

"That's it. They say he could talk all nice and get anyone to believe him. And then they'd just hand over their money."

Bea slipped an arm around Lucy's waist and pulled her close. She breathed through the contact, not wanting to offend Bea because she never meant any harm. But her arm had the strength of iron and she held Lucy tightly against her as they walked. Even as they went up the steps of the café, Bea held tight.

"I'm sure glad you're home," Bea repeated as they entered the café. "Apparently you won't stay. But I think you might. Because folks in Bluebonnet are real good people. Did you know those Helping Hands people came and mowed my lawn today? The church isn't like it was when your daddy ran it. No, these days the people are real kind and they say the Bible says to love your neighbor as yourself and that we have to practice what the Bible tells us."

"Hey, neighbor," a voice called out from behind her.

Dane appeared at her side. He grinned at her and pulled off his sunglasses.

"Why, Dane Scott, you sure are good-looking." Bea whistled and gave him a once-over. "I sure like them Wrangler jeans you're wearing. And did you know we're supposed to love our neighbor?"

"Why, yes, Bea, I was aware of that. Did you know that Lucy Palermo is my neighbor?"

Bea whistled again. "That sure is awkward. I don't think it means to love her like that, Dane. I reckon my mama wouldn't have liked that kind of talk."

He kissed Bea on the cheek and she turned bright red.

"Bea, I do apologize."

Bea walked off muttering about sin and good-looking men.

"Are you having lunch?" Dane asked, tagging along as Lucy headed for a table.

"I am having lunch. Are you here to cause trouble?" She sat down and he parked himself across from her.

"I'm not here to cause trouble." He picked up a menu and glanced over it. "I just thought I'd be neighborly. Isn't that what Bea was talking about?"

"I don't think so."

The front door opened and several men entered the restaurant. Bea hurried out of the kitchen to greet them. Lucy closed her eyes.

"Wait for it. Wait for it," Dane said with a wide grin on his face.

"Stop it."

"Pastor Matthews!" Bea hurried to the pastor's side. "Did you know that Dane loves his neighbor? I think you should talk to him about that verse because you say that we aren't to use God's word inappropriately, for our own purpose."

Lucy made eye contact with the man across from her. "I tried to warn you."

He pointed to himself and made a mockery of looking chastised. "I still think she is misinterpreting what I meant."

Lucy pointed at him. "Quiet, you."

Pastor Matthews, Chet and several others picked the table next to Lucy and Dane. She skewered him with a look that she hoped would keep him quiet.

"Dane, it seems we need to discuss the meaning of the verse 'Love thy neighbor.'" Pastor Matthews looked from Dane to Lucy. "To interpret that correctly, we need to care about the people that come into our lives. We need to show compassion and charity."

"Pastor, that's exactly what I'm trying to do. Lucy, could I buy you lunch?"

"No."

Dane raised his hands in defeat. "Do you see? I tried to show charity."

Pastor Matthews grinned big and Lucy knew from that look that Dane had fallen into a trap of his own making.

"It's good that you're feeling charitable," the pastor started. "We've been mowing lawns for some people who are unable. After lunch I'm heading back to the shelter to work on the stair railing outside. It's loose and I wouldn't want someone to grab hold of it and fall. A guy with a charitable nature might want to help out."

Dane glanced at his watch. "I've got Doc Adams at my place this afternoon to work calves but I'm game to help if you need my lack of expertise."

The pastor winked at Lucy, then he got out of his chair and joined them. "You know I'll take whatever labor I can find."

The pastor put a hand on her shoulder. She stiffened beneath his touch. Dane caught and held her gaze, his expression going soft and kind.

"Lucy, I wanted to thank you for the work on the security system. It definitely works. It was set and I forgot about it."

"Caught you by surprise, did it?" Dane asked, his gaze still focused on Lucy.

"It did. But we know it works, and so do the county deputies." As the pastor glanced back at the table of men he'd come in with, his hand slipped off her shoulder. "I'd best get over there and keep those men out of trouble. I think I just heard Essie growl at one of them."

"Always best to stay on her good side," Dane offered.

"I'm always good to the person cooking my food. Dane, I'll see you later. Lucy, again, I appreciate your help."

The pastor walked away. Dane picked up the menu and quickly scanned it, even though he knew the offerings like the back of his hand. "You okay?"

Lucy turned her coffee cup right side up for the waitress, who was making a beeline for their table.

"Of course I am."

The waitress filled their coffee cups and left. Essie joined them, her hair pulled back but strands coming loose and curling around her face. She looked frazzled but Lucy wasn't about to point that out. With a sigh, Lucy's aunt sat down.

"Goodness, they didn't even wipe this table down." She swiped crumbs into her hand. "Lucy, what are you having?"

Lucy glanced up at the whiteboard near the register. The daily specials were written in red marker. Desserts were written in black.

"Pecan pie," she said. "And an order of fries."

"That isn't lunch!" Her aunt didn't look at all amused. "A chef salad it is."

Dane put the menu back in its spot between the napkin holder and the sugar dish.

"Dane, what'll you have?" Essie held her pen to the pad in her hand. Her lips were in a firm line as she waited.

"I think I'm going with the safe choice."

Essie arched one brow. "Which is…"

"I'm going to let you choose and save myself a lecture."

Essie pointed a finger at him. "I choose for you to remain silent."

Lucy tiptoed into the fray. "Essie, is everything okay?"

"Of course it is. Why?"

"You seem grouchier than normal," Chet replied from the other table, proving he didn't have any sense.

"Just for that, you get split pea soup. I know it's your favorite, old man." She tapped her pen on the order pad.

"Oh, come on, Essie, you know I was only joking." Chet made a sweet face that probably wouldn't do him a bit of good. "Why don't you tell us what's wrong? Maybe we can help."

"All right, fine. My cat died last night." She avoided eye contact with Lucy as she gave the explanation. "I've had that cat for fifteen years."

"Oh, now, Essie, don't you go and start acting all human on me. You'll make me cry. I'm always a sympathetic crier." Chet reached over and patted her back with a large, calloused hand. "If it'll make you smile, I'll get you a kitten."

"I don't want a kitten, you cantankerous old man." Essie reached for a napkin and wiped her eyes. "Okay, lunch is on me. Because I'm sorry for being such a grouch."

"Don't even think about it, Essie. I'll pay," Dane offered. "My condolences. I am sorry about your cat. If it makes you feel better, I'll take a chef salad, also. And pecan pie."

As Essie wrote down Dane's order, Lucy studied her aunt closely. She knew what the others obviously didn't. Essie didn't have a cat. She was allergic.

Suddenly a foot hit hers. She glanced at Dane and he winked. To avoid getting drawn in, she picked up the menu and pretended to study it. She didn't want to feel connected to him. But sometimes it felt like there was nothing she could do to stop it.

Dane Scott was starting to be irresistible.

"Essie has never owned a cat in her life," Lucy revealed to Dane after they'd left Essie's.

"I didn't think she was a cat owner. So why the story?"

"I'm not sure. I guess I'll ask her later. I need to get home and get some work done. Alex is buying cattle. It seems he's had some decent winnings this year."

Dane wondered why a man on a winning streak would walk away from a sport that he loved right when he seemed to be making decent money.

As they passed the feed store, a few of the men called out to them, waving. They were known as the "liars club." Local men who met at the feed store for free coffee and gossip. Mandy Williams owned the feed store with her husband. She didn't mind donating the coffee, but if the gossip crossed the line or the language got too salty she made them put a dollar in the coffee donation box.

"Hey, Lucy. Come up here for a sec."

Lucy waved at Tommy Murray, a neighbor to the west of the Palermos. But she didn't look like she planned on stopping to talk.

"Might as well see what he wants."

She sighed, but then headed back toward the feed store and the men sitting on the concrete loading dock.

"Hey, Tommy, don't you have work to do on your place." Dane reached to shake hands with Tommy and the others.

Tommy Murray, comfortable on the bench, a cup of coffee in his hands, nodded as he looked at Lucy. "Remember that little mare of mine that you used to sneak over and ride?"

She nodded. "I didn't know you knew about that."

"Oh, you weren't as sneaky as you thought. I saw you a time or two back in the trees. I wouldn't have said anything to get you in trouble."

"She was a nice mare," Lucy responded.

"She was. And she threw some nice foals. I have a little mare, about five years old, out of that mare. Her sire was a gray Arabian."

"I see."

"I thought since you're home, you might like to buy her."

"I don't know about buying a horse, but thank you."

"Well, isn't Alex home and buying livestock?" Tommy quizzed, raising his glasses to give her a hard stare. "I just assumed you were home for good."

"I haven't really made a plan." She looked at Dane, then her gaze darted away and he wondered. He wondered why she wouldn't look at him and he wondered why it should matter to him so much.

She didn't owe him an explanation. Neither of them were responsible to the other. He had his place up for sale. She had made it clear she was just here for Maria. When it came to being unequally yoked, the two of them were poster children.

"Well, keep her in mind," Tommy was saying. He was a horse trader and he rarely backed down. "I'm going to put her on my website but I thought if you wanted her, I'd give you the first shot at her. She's a pretty grullo, like her mama."

Temptation with hooves. Dane knew Lucy well enough to know she wanted that horse the way some women wanted diamonds. "I might come by and look at her," she admitted.

"That'd be fine."

They said their goodbyes and walked away. Dane maintained a safe distance between them. She wanted that mare, he could tell.

"Another horse feels like a commitment to stay, huh?" he asked as they got closer to her truck.

"Yes, something like that."

He understood. She didn't want to be tied down to Bluebonnet. And he'd known that since the very beginning. Since the first day when she'd stood at the side of the road looking down at her sister's truck lodged in his fence.

At least she was honest. He wasn't quite ready for all that honesty, though. Not even with himself.

She touched his arm, just a brief touch. "I'll meet you at the church. I'm going to say hello to a couple of the ladies."

"I'll see you there."

He watched her walk away and halfway to her car she glanced back at him, frowning when she saw that he was still standing there. He waved and she shook her head. Taking the hint he climbed behind the wheel of his truck and headed the few blocks to the church.

Before he got there he saw the flashing blue lights. Patrol cars were pulling in to the driveway of the church. A few of the women were outside. Dane parked and got out. Lucy was almost immediately at his side.

Pastor Matthews came out the front door of the building and the deputies joined him. When he saw Dane and Lucy, he waved them over.

"What happened?" Lucy asked as they approached.

"Willa came back yesterday. About thirty minutes ago her husband caught her in the yard playing with their little boy."

"Is the suspect still on the premises?" one of the deputies asked, his hand going to his sidearm.

"No, he left," Pastor Matthews answered, his expression troubled. "He went east."

"Do you have a description of the car?" The deputy listened to the response and called in the BOLO on the car and the suspect. He excused himself to talk to the women who had witnessed the attack.

"Can I see Willa?" Lucy asked.

Pastor Matthews looked to the deputy, who nodded. "She's inside with the city officer."

"She's pretty beat up, Lucy." Pastor Matthews pointed toward the door. "My wife has been with her."

"Is she going to need medical care?" Lucy asked.

"She said no, but I think she might have a cracked rib and probably a broken nose."

"What about her little boy, Seth?" Lucy asked as they entered the church.

"He's okay. She had him run inside when she saw her husband pull up." Pastor Matthews responded as he walked next to her.

Dane had followed. Lucy knew how to take care of herself. She didn't need him to protect her, but he wanted to be with her. Things appeared calm but he worried that Willa's husband might come back and if he did, Dane didn't want Lucy to be alone.

He thought she'd probably been alone too often in life.

Chapter Eleven

The police officer met them at the door to the shelter. He unlocked it and told them he would be there if they needed him. Lucy thanked him as she stepped inside, Dane at her back. They walked down the dimly lit hall, Pastor Matthews leading the way.

She stopped walking and reached for Dane's arm. He glanced down, questions in his eyes as she stood there, trying to find words to explain this situation.

"You should wait in the fellowship hall," she told him. "The women are going to be nervous and your presence won't help. I'm sorry."

Kindness lit his blue eyes. "I understand. There's no need to be sorry. But I'm here if you need me, not that I expect that to happen."

The comment changed everything. "Thank you."

"Anytime. But if you ever do need me to ride to the rescue, just say the word."

"Okay," she whispered, then felt silly. She didn't do silly or weak.

She didn't need a man to rescue her. She'd been rescuing herself for a long time. She'd survived her father. She'd survived an IED in Afghanistan. The man standing in front of her would not be her knight in shining armor.

But she'd just said *okay*, as if she meant for him to rescue her right then. And the soft glimmer of understanding in his eyes nearly undid her.

His hand touched hers. Barely. The touch so soft, so gentle, she hardly knew if it had happened.

"Go," she told him.

He saluted her and walked down the hall. Lucy watched him go, then she forced herself to move. Pastor Matthews had left the two of them alone but she could hear his steady, calming voice coming from a room down the hall.

There were three women in the room that Lucy entered a few seconds later. Willa was seated on a chair. One of the women from the shelter stood nearby holding a first aid kit. The other woman lived in Bluebonnet. Her name was Elaine and she'd worked at the grocery store for as long as Lucy could remember.

"Hey, Willa." Lucy approached the three, a gentle smile for Willa.

"Lucy," Willa sobbed, tears running down her bruised and battered cheeks. "I cooked the wrong kind of beans. I knew it, but it was all we had."

"Willa, don't make excuses for him," Lucy said gently but inside she felt like screaming. Why did abusers always make their victims feel as if the blame was on them? "Where's Seth?"

"He's in the nursery. Johnny smacked him pretty hard. But I think he's okay."

"Oh, Willa." Lucy squatted in front of the broken woman. "I'd like to take you to the doctor. We want to make sure nothing is broken."

Elaine situated an ice pack on Willa's busted nose. "She said it hurts to move and taking a deep breath is painful."

"He kicked me," Willa said. "I was moving away from him and I grabbed a stick so he couldn't hit me again. So he kicked me."

She said it half-proud but sobbed as she finished the tale.

"Willa, your little boy needs you healthy. I'll take you to the doctor here in town. We'll get you and Seth checked out. My neighbor is going with us, just so nothing else can happen to you."

Willa closed her eyes, then she nodded once. "Okay."

Lucy took the first aid kit from the woman standing at Willa's side. She opened a bandage and applied salve.

"I'm going to put this on your face, because there's a cut on your cheek. Okay?"

Willa nodded and silent tears dripped down her cheeks again. She flinched when the bandage touched the gash. The moment brought back a memory of her mother doing the same for her. That day, when her father had beat her with a riding crop, had changed everything for Lucy. She remembered it so vividly, even though she'd been only fourteen at the time. She'd told her mom that someday she'd leave and she wouldn't come back. She'd promised her mom that she would never get married because no man would ever control her. Her mom had told her to hush and don't start more trouble.

As if she had started the trouble. She'd looked at her dad the wrong way and for that she'd had to write Scripture, and then she'd accidentally misquoted a verse. For

Jesse Palermo it hadn't been about the Bible or God. It had been about control and power.

"I don't know what I'll do without him." Willa spoke as Lucy finished cleaning her face.

"One day at a time," Lucy told her. "Each day you'll get stronger. Each day you'll feel better. Each day you'll feel safer."

The words were the greatest truth she'd ever spoken. Each day after leaving her home and her family, Lucy had grown stronger. She'd felt more in control of her own life, her own future.

She wouldn't give that control to anyone else.

Willa drew in a deep breath, tears filling her eyes. "I do need a doctor."

"Yes, you do. I'll take you to our local doctor."

"Thank you, Lucy," Willa whispered in a small voice as she pushed to her feet.

They found Dane in the fellowship hall. He was leaning against the counter, a cup of coffee in his hands. Lucy faltered a bit as she approached him. Her pledge to always be strong seemed to hit a brick wall because he made her feel weak.

She glanced away from him, because she'd been staring and felt as if she didn't know herself at that moment. She remembered back, telling her mother she'd never let a man control her. She'd meant the way her father controlled people. But now she knew that there were other ways men controlled. Ways she hadn't expected, ways that didn't necessarily feel dangerous. At least not dangerous in the way she'd always feared.

Pastor Matthews stepped forward, holding a cup of coffee out to Willa. Seth, Willa's two-year-old son, came flying into the room, his face dirty and bruises already coloring his fair cheeks. Lucy grabbed him up before he could plow into his mom.

"Hey, Seth, remember me?" she asked as she held on to him. He stopped trying to escape. "We're going to take you and your mom for a drive. But first I'm going to see if there are any cookies around here. Want a cookie?"

The little boy nodded. Lucy headed for the kitchen but Dane had heard and he was already there, rummaging through the cabinets. By the time they reached him he'd found a chocolate chip cookie and a cream-filled cookie. He handed them both Seth.

"How about two cookies?" Dane asked.

Seth took the cookies, and then he reached for Dane. Lucy let go, because she knew that Dane had experience with kids. She had never seen herself as soft and comforting.

"We pulled the truck up to the back of the church." Dane held Seth in one arm. "I'll drive if you want to get Willa."

"Sounds good," she said. She walked back to the fellowship hall.

Pastor Matthews took Willa gingerly by the arm. "Let's take it slow and easy as we walk out there."

"What if Johnny comes back here?" Willa asked as they walked to the truck. She looked around nervously, her gaze anxiously seeking him out.

Lucy remained close to Willa's side but she glanced back at Dane and Seth. She didn't want the little guy to be worried, thinking his daddy might return. Dane was keeping him busy talking to him. Lucy opened the truck door for Willa.

"The deputy is going to follow us, Willa." Lucy helped the other woman get settled. "But you have to press charges. The safest thing for you is to put Johnny behind bars."

Willa shook her head at the suggestion. "I don't think I can press charges against my husband."

Lucy had expected that. "I know you think that. But you can. And you should."

Willa eased herself into the truck, her face tight with pain. "Where will I be when Johnny gets here?"

"I have an apartment in Austin. It's sitting empty and the rent is paid. I'll take you there this weekend. If you'll go."

Willa studied the sky as if she'd never before seen that shade of blue. Lucy didn't press her for an answer. She'd either take the help or she wouldn't.

Doc Parker had an office in a convenience store that had closed down. He lived in the back, drove an old Jeep and said he was saving money for retirement. But he was seventy if he was a day and Lucy guessed he would never retire. When he saw Willa, he shook his head and pointed to the exam table.

"Looks as if you've had a rough day." He touched the cut on her head, and then moved on to her nose. "I'm going to have you lay back on the exam table. Now don't you worry. Lucy won't leave and I'll be gentle. Dane is in the waiting room with your little boy. I think they're playing one of them silly games on the smartphone. Technology. It sure has changed since I was your age. We used to hunt for dimes to use the pay phone."

He kept talking, his voice low and soothing, as he did his exam. Willa cried the entire time.

"Nothing broken." He paused, his expression growing gentle. "When did you lose the baby?"

Willa started to sob. Lucy held her hand tight and blinked back tears because Willa didn't need her sympathy. She needed someone strong, holding her hand and telling her it would be okay.

"He kicked me and knocked me down." Her voice trembled.

"In the past week or two?"

Willa nodded. "I couldn't stop it from happening."

"No, I reckon you couldn't. Now, you listen to me. Your body needs to heal. But you've got other healing to do, too. Your emotions. Your mind and the way you see yourself. Those things need to heal. When you leave here, I want you to think about getting some help for the emotional hurts so those can heal."

He patted her arm, then he helped her sit.

"Thank you, Doctor."

"You're welcome, honey." He pulled up a chair and sat down. "I lost my only child to a situation like yours. She didn't leave him, and in the end he killed her. I want you to live, Willa. You deserve to live."

She nodded and tears flowed down her cheeks. Doc Parker handed her a box of tissues but he pulled one out for Lucy and one for himself.

Lucy stood there holding that tissue, her eyes dry but her throat tight. When Doc Parker asked Willa if he could pray, Lucy wasn't surprised. She bowed her head and listened as he asked God to guide Willa, to keep her safe and to help them all to find healing in all areas of their lives.

If she hadn't felt compelled to stay in Bluebonnet for her little sister, she might have jumped in her truck and driven off into the proverbial sunset to escape the emotions that were battering at her heart.

But she had promised Maria. So she stood there in Doc Parker's office, praying for Willa. Praying for her sister. And praying for herself.

* * *

When they got back to the church, Dane watched as Lucy loaded Willa and Seth into her truck. She'd made the plan on the way back from Doc's to take Willa home with her to the ranch. Dane wasn't thrilled with the idea, but he knew he didn't have a say.

That didn't mean he wouldn't try to talk her out of it. Once she had Willa and Seth loaded, she walked back to where he stood leaning against his truck. Before he'd even had a chance to say anything, she gave him a look that told him she didn't want his advice or interference. He was going to disappoint her.

"I know you can take care of yourself," he started.

"And I know that you believe that," she replied. "Dane, I'm fully capable of keeping Willa safe. It's what I do for a living. I protect people. She'll be safer with me than she will at the church. And the women at the church will be safer because she won't be there. A complaint has been filed. They have a warrant for Johnny's arrest. Willa is taking steps to make sure he doesn't hurt her again."

"I know." But he realized he had to admit what he really felt. Deep down felt. The confession was as much for him as it was for her. "I don't want you to get hurt, Lucy."

Her eyes widened as she looked up at him, and for the first time she didn't have a ready response.

"I know, I'm speechless, too," he teased.

"I have to go." She shook free when he tried to reach for her hand. "No. Don't."

"I'm too old for games, Lucy. I'm not going to pretend that I'm not attracted to you or that I don't enjoy being around you. I'm also going to be honest and tell you that I wasn't looking for a relationship."

She didn't look up at him. "I know you're not. And neither am I. Which is a pretty good reason for us to keep things in perspective. Once upon a time a lost girl thought you would save her, and then she realized she could save herself. I'm not that girl anymore."

"I know you're not. And I've got my own baggage, too."

"We're moving in opposite directions, you and I," she reminded him. "I have a business that I love. You're trying to sell your ranch."

"All valid points," he said.

"I have to get Willa to the house," Lucy retorted.

"I know you do. And I've got to get home and work cattle. But, like it or not, I'll be by later to check on you."

"You don't have to do that, Dane."

"No, I don't. But I'm going to, anyway."

He walked her to her truck. Their shoulders touched and he let his hand brush against hers. When she didn't protest, he slid his fingers through hers. Baby steps. For both of them.

"I'll see you later," he told her as he opened her truck door.

"Go home," she commanded with a not so subtle glare. "You have a daughter who needs you." She climbed behind the wheel and he closed the door.

He watched until the truck was safely on the road, and then he walked back to the church. Pastor Matthews was waiting for him. "Did you see them off?"

"Yes." He hoped there weren't more questions to follow that one. Difficult questions he wasn't quite ready to find answers for.

"Where's Issy?"

Dane sat down at the table, across from the pastor.

"She's with Haven. They went to Dallas to visit our folks."

"Do you think Willa is safe at Lucy's? I can have the local deputy take a drive by the Palermo ranch."

"I think Lucy would hate that. But then, what she doesn't know can't make her mad."

"That's a good motto. I'll let the county guys know." Pastor Matthews headed for the door. "I have a wife who is going to send out a search party if I don't get home."

Dane turned off lights as he walked out the door. "I'm sure your wife will be glad to see you. Even if you have caused her a lot of grief."

Pastor Matthews laughed. "You're an encourager, Dane."

"I do my best. See you later."

On his way home, Dane took the side road that led past the Palermo ranch. The drive was long but he could see the dark silhouette of the house, a few lights glowing yellow in the windows. He slowed, watching for anything out of place, anything that didn't make sense.

The only thing that didn't make sense was that he was sitting at the end of the road looking at her house, worrying about her.

But all he knew was that since she'd come home, he'd felt a lot less alone than he'd felt for the past couple of years. That had to mean something, didn't it?

Chapter Twelve

The smell of bacon frying and coffee brewing woke Lucy from a deep sleep. She forced herself out of bed and down the hall to the kitchen. The sun was barely over the eastern horizon but Maria and Willa were at the stove, talking quietly and making breakfast. Maria waved a spatula when she saw Lucy.

Her sister, her baby bump more obvious in a tight T-shirt, stood next to Willa with a spatula in hand. For years Lucy had lived a very solitary life. She could admit now that it had been more selfish than solitary. She hadn't wanted to be here, hadn't wanted to be involved with her family. Keeping to herself had meant not getting pulled in to the needs of others.

It had always felt safer that way.

Now she called it what it was. Lonely.

"Coffee is done and breakfast will be ready in a few minutes."

Lucy glared at her cheerful little sister. "How is it I didn't know you cook?"

Maria flipped eggs and gave Willa a conspiratorial look. "I wasn't trying to hide it from you. I just thought you should work on your own cooking skills. I didn't know how that would affect me, though."

Lucy poured coffee and glanced toward the living room. "Did you know Isabelle is sleeping on our couch?"

"No way? Really?" Maria slid eggs onto a plate.

"Yes, I know she's there. It isn't as if we have a cat burglar who brings small children and leaves them. Dane is moving cattle this morning. And then he wants to use our bush hog."

"And Issy?"

"She and Haven got back from Dallas late last night, then Haven got called in for an extra shift."

Lucy watched as the child moved on the couch, drawing a blanket up to her chin and putting her thumb into her mouth. "How are you this morning, Willa? And Seth?"

"We're real good, Miss Lucy. And thank you again for taking us in like this. We haven't slept so good in a long time."

"I'm glad to hear that. Just make yourself at home and let me know if you need anything." She returned her attention to her sister. "Where's Alex?"

"Still in Stephenville."

She nodded, accepting the information. "And how are you feeling?"

"I wasn't sick this morning." Maria handed her a plate. "Eat."

"I'm not a breakfast person." But she had to admit the food looked good. She accepted the fork her sister offered and took a bite. "I'm also not cooking another meal."

Maria looked pleased as she headed for the table with her own plate. Lucy joined them. It was hard to sit at that table and not think back to all the silent meals with their father at the head of the table. She must have glanced at his empty seat because Maria cleared her throat and tapped the table in front of Lucy.

"What?" Lucy asked, getting up to refill her coffee. Everyone else in the Palermo family might like to avoid the topic, but not Maria. The past. Their family. All topics were fair game.

"You have to let it go. Forgive him because if you don't, it'll eat you alive."

"Says the eighteen-year-old." Lucy refilled her cup, regretting the harsh words as soon as they left her mouth. "Sorry, that wasn't fair. You're a much wiser person at eighteen than I am at twenty-nine."

"That goes without saying." Maria grinned, but the gesture dissolved into a serious look. "Lucy, I know he's gone and I know you have bad memories, but forgiving him will help you move past this."

"We have company right now and she doesn't want to hear our family stories."

Willa, her hair pulled back from her bruised and broken face, shrugged. "I don't really mind. I guess it makes us a sisterhood. We're survivors."

"Yes, I guess we are." Lucy carried her plate to the sink and headed for the back door. "I've got to feed, and then I'm going to work on the garden. Did Chuck Nash come over yesterday to till it?"

Maria, mouth full of egg, nodded. Lucy headed out the back door, eager to be in the fresh air and sunshine. She breathed in deep and looked up at the deep blue sky dotted with puffy white clouds. If God was out there, she wondered if He realized how much she appreciated a perfect morning such as this.

She also wondered if it had been God's plan to bring

her back here and make her confront not just her past, but the life she'd been living. A life she'd been perfectly happy with, or so she thought.

Because she hadn't truly been happy. When this was all over maybe she'd go back to her job and her life with a different perspective.

Or she'd return to Austin and be homesick. For the first time ever.

After lunch Lucy led Issy to the garden so they could take advantage of the unseasonably cool day. Issy held tight to her hand as they crossed the yard and jabbered about kittens, puppies and the pony.

"I wonder if there are little saddles for little ponies." Issy said it softly, almost to herself.

"I know there are little saddles. We have one in the barn. It's just the right size for a pony like Cobalt."

"Is it the right size for little girls?"

Lucy smiled down at the child. "It is definitely the right size."

When they got to the garden spot, Lucy spread an old blanket on the ground under a tree.

"Issy, you sit here with your baby doll. I'm going to get the plants for the garden."

"Are there apple plants?" Issy asked.

"No apples," she said as she sat down next to the child. "But there are cucumbers, tomatoes and green beans. Apples grow on trees."

"Oh." Issy's little mouth turned down in disappointment. "I like apples."

"Me, too." Lucy pushed to her feet. "I'll be right back."

A door banged shut. Lucy glanced toward the house. Willa waved and headed their way. She was walking slowly, her hand to her side, but she was smiling. She met Lucy at the shed.

"Seth is taking a nap so I thought I'd help you out." She looked down at the jeans and T-shirt she wore. "I hope you don't mind. Maria found something of yours for me to wear. We're about the same size. Maria is a little taller."

"I don't mind at all." Lucy handed her a tray of plants. "But I don't want you to overdo it. I know your ribs are only bruised but you've been through a lot."

Willa's expression fell and her eyes glazed over. "Yes, well, today is a new day. I haven't worn pants in a long time. Johnny wouldn't let me."

"Well, Johnny isn't here to tell you that you can't."

"No, I reckon he isn't." Willa followed her to the garden. "Is there a church near where that apartment is?" Willa asked as they made a second trip for shovels and tomato cages.

"I'm sure there is. I've never really looked. There's a small community college nearby, Willa. You might want to take some classes."

"I might do that. I made good grades in school." She picked up a hoe and started making rows in the garden. "I always wanted to be a nurse. Guess I wanted it, but I didn't believe I could do it."

"I think you can do anything you put your mind to."

"I'm not so sure. It scares me, just thinking about walking away from Johnny. I guess as bad as life was at home, and then with my husband, at least I had people. At least I knew what to expect."

"It's frightening to step into the unknown." Lucy handed her a set of tomato plants for the holes she'd dug. "What was your home like, Willa?"

"It wasn't always bad." Willa chewed on her bottom

lip as she thought of an answer. "I grew up outside of Killeen. My parents worked and sometimes they would take us to the park or the lake. But they were drunks. Mean drunks. And then I married a mean drunk. As much as I said I would escape that life, I married and just kept right on living the nightmare."

"But now you're making an effort to break away," Lucy encouraged. "Sometimes it's about having support."

"Support and a lot of faith," Willa told her. "Johnny can have the stuff. What he can't have is me. He can't take my pride. Or my life. And he can't take my faith."

Moved beyond words, Lucy stepped forward and hugged the other woman gingerly. "Willa, you might think I'm strong, but you've got me beat."

When Lucy had run away from home she'd also run away from her faith. She'd left it in this house with all of the other bad memories. Willa might feel as if she was the one being helped but Lucy had just been given a lesson in letting go.

They returned to the garden and the conversation turned to lighter topics. Willa made straight rows while Lucy started digging holes for the plants. Issy had tired of playing on the blanket and she sat next to Lucy, occasionally testing the depth of a hole with tiny fingers.

After digging a row and planting several tomato plants, Willa stood and tentatively touched her side. "I think I'm done."

"You should definitely rest." Lucy handed Issy a tomato plant. "Issy and I can finish up out here."

"I'll rest, and then I'll see what Maria and I can do about supper."

"You don't have to do that, Willa," Lucy assured the other woman.

"But I want to. It makes me feel better if I have something to do. And I have an aunt who says I can come stay with her. What would you think of that? I'm afraid if I'm alone, the minute Johnny calls, I'll go back."

Lucy smoothed the curls of the little girl sitting next to her. "I think that sounds wise. The most important thing is that you do what's best for yourself and for Seth."

"I think it's best."

"We'll do whatever we can to help you."

Then Willa left, walking slow and holding her side as she crossed the yard.

Issy tugged on Lucy's sleeve. "Is there a watermelon?"

Lucy looked over the plants. "I don't think so. But if they have plants at the feed store, I'll get one and plant it for you. Do you want to plant these tomatoes?"

Issy nodded. "Yes. I like to plant gardens."

Lucy placed the small tomato plant in her little hands. Issy pushed her nose into the plant.

"I like the way it smells."

"Really?" Lucy leaned to take whiff. "Interesting. Do you like the way it feels?"

She guided Issy's hands to gently touch the leaves and stems.

"Yes, but I like the smell better."

Lucy guided her to the hole in the soil for the plant. "It will have flowers on it. Tiny flowers that become little tomatoes."

Issy settled the plant in the hole, then they brushed soil around it. "Will we water the plants?"

"Yes, we will. Plants need a lot of water to grow."

Issy patted the soil around the plant. "And little girls need hugs to grow."

"Yes, they do," Lucy agreed.

The little girl grinned up at her. "My daddy told me so."

Then Issy stood, wrapped her arms around Lucy's neck and hugged her tight.

Dane walked around the corner of the house and spotted Lucy and Issy in the garden. He stopped to watch as his daughter patted soil around a plant she'd just placed in the ground. Lucy spoke to her and Issy hopped to her feet and wrapped her arms around Lucy's neck.

His little girl needed those hugs. Lucy had a deep down kindness. She appeared distant and even cool at times, but she cared about the people in her life. She cared about little girls. She cared about women who needed protection and a fresh start. She cared a lot.

Issy might never know that kind of caring from her own mother. Tamara might visit. There might be lunches or even meetings at a park. But he didn't see Issy's mom taking on the role of mother that she had rejected three years ago.

Lucy spotted him. She said something to Issy and his daughter raised her hand to wave. He headed their way, watching as they eased another plant into the ground and Issy pushed soil around the roots.

"You girls look like you're working hard." He reached for a plant and knelt next to his daughter.

"Daddy, do you want to help?" Issy touched his arm. "We might plant watermelons."

"Really?" He looked to Lucy for confirmation. A garden was a commitment. If a person planted a garden, didn't that mean they planned to stay and tend the plants, harvest them in the fall?

"Yes, we are." Lucy sat back on her heels and

watched as he helped his daughter with the next couple of plants.

"I got a call from the sheriff. Johnny is now their guest." He said it in a way that he hoped wouldn't worry his daughter.

"That's good. I'm sure he'll enjoy the stay." Lucy smiled down at his daughter. "That means it will be okay for Willa to grab a few things that are special to her before she moves. She's decided to move in with an aunt."

"If you need help, let me know. We can always take a trailer to load up whatever she wants to keep."

"I'll ask her." Lucy started gathering up the garden tools. "I think I'll take her Sunday afternoon. She wants to go to church here before she leaves."

"I'll keep my schedule open."

"Thank you."

Dane reached for the green beans. "We might as well finish."

Lucy reached for a tray of plants. "I guess we can. Did you still need the bush hog?"

"Yeah, I'm trying to reclaim fifty acres that has gone to weeds."

The sun beat down on them as they finished a row of beans. Issy tugged on his sleeve. "Daddy, I'm sleepy and thirsty."

"We've been out here awhile." Lucy wiped dirt off her hands. "Issy is probably ready to go inside with Maria and Princess the rotten poodle."

"If you take her in, I'll keep planting." Dane never put in a garden but the idea might be growing on him because of Lucy. Yeah, because of Lucy.

"Then I'll take Issy inside to Maria." Lucy lifted the little girl into her arms.

He reached for another tray, but then he sat back and stretched. "Mind getting me a glass of water while you're in there? I don't quit, but I do like a break from time to time."

Lucy held Issy close. "Says the man who just got here five minutes ago."

He laughed. "I didn't say I was working hard."

After they'd walked away he headed for the outside spigot attached to a garden hose. He pulled the handle and unwound the hose to drag it to the garden. The new plants needed watering. And so did he. He ran water in his hand and splashed his face, then rinsed his hands and arms before turning the hose on the garden.

"Feel better?"

Lucy appeared at his side, grinning as she slid her gaze over his wet hair and face.

"Actually, yes." He turned the hose on her and she ran, but not before he got her. "Do you feel better?"

She swiped at the water dripping down her face. "That was unkind. And after I brought you a bottle of cold water."

"You're right. Very unkind." He dropped the hose and went after her but she ran, taking both bottles of water with her.

Halfway across the yard he caught her, pulling her back against his chest as she fought to escape. "Caught you."

"Now what do you plan to do?"

Water still dripped from her hair, down her cheek. That was about the most intriguing drop of water he'd ever seen. But then, she was the most intriguing female he'd ever known. He held her and she didn't seem in a hurry to escape. Instead she was soft in his arms, leaning a little against his shoulder.

She brought out the worst in him. Or maybe the best. It felt good to hold her and it felt good to laugh. For a few minutes he didn't want to think about either of them leaving. For a few minutes he'd like to go back and just be kids from Bluebonnet on a summer day. Even if they were long past being kids.

"Well?" she asked, her expression softening.

"I'm going to do this." He leaned, kissing that drop of water from her cheek. Then he moved to her mouth.

"And this," he said. He buried his hands in the soft waves of her brown hair and held her close to kiss her the way he'd wanted to for days. He wanted her to stay. He wanted to recapture perfect summer days, when she'd been his for just a few short weeks.

But he wouldn't say it out loud because once he did it would be hers to reject, to tell him why it wouldn't work. If he said it, he'd have to take a closer look and he might find that what they'd had was gone and this was just another stolen moment. So he kissed her until she wiggled out of his arms and shot a cautious look in the direction of the field.

"That would be Essie," she whispered. She exhaled and looked up at him. "That was your plan?"

"I didn't really think it through."

"Maybe we should have given it more thought."

He shook his head, disagreeing. "No, because then we would have walked away and we wouldn't have had that moment."

She stared up at him. "Moments don't last."

"Sometimes they do." He pushed damp hair back from her face. "Go to church with us tomorrow."

She blinked a few times and shook her head. "What? Why?"

"It's important to me. Just go with us?"

Before she could respond, Essie was there, getting off her ATV, giving them a long look as she pulled off her helmet and hung it over the handlebars of the vehicle.

"Well, well, well." Essie looked from one of them to the other and Dane felt a lot like a teenager caught on a back road. "I called and Maria said you were gardening. That's the most interesting form of gardening I think I've ever seen."

Lucy cleared her throat and stepped forward to hug her aunt. "Essie, what are up to today? Maria made lemonade if you'd care for some."

"Uh-huh, that's how we're going to play this?" Essie sat down on the seat of the ATV. "I came over to bring you a gift."

The older woman reached into the basket on the back of the ATV. She pulled out a little gray kitten and practically tossed it to Lucy.

"A kitten?" Lucy held the squirming, hissing feline. "I don't want a cat."

"Funny," Essie said, her accent heavier than usual. "I didn't want a cat, either. But Chet showed up this morning with a kitten for me. He was real sad that I'd lost my cat and he thought this little kitten would make me happy."

"What a sweet thing to do," Lucy cooed, then she handed the kitten to Dane. He took it, but he definitely didn't want it.

Essie's eyes narrowed as she stared her niece down. "I don't like cats and you know that. But it seems that Chet was told a kitten might make me happy."

"And it didn't?" Lucy asked, all innocence. Dane laughed, which earned him a stare down from Essie.

"Not really." A hint of a smile curved Essie's lips. "I wasn't upset about a cat."

"No?"

Essie glared at the kitten in Dane's arms. "No. But what woman wants to admit she's attached to a stupid rooster. I've had that rooster for three years. He was on my porch every morning, crowing in the new day."

"Not Rooster Cogburn," Lucy cried out, obviously distressed. Dane was lost.

"A coyote got him." Essie said it with a trace of the previous day's sadness. "I really liked that rooster."

"Oh, Aunt Essie, I am so sorry." Lucy leaned to hug her aunt and they awkwardly patted each other on the back. Over a rooster. Dane looked at the kitten that had curled up to sleep on his shoulder.

"Looks like the kitten has a home." Essie beamed, proud of herself. "Issy will love that kitten."

Great, a kitten. A phone rang before he could explain that the last thing they needed was a cat. Lucy reached into her pocket and walked away, phone to her ear. The conversation was serious but he couldn't make out what was being said. Essie didn't seem to be bothered by it. She kept talking about her rooster and how she'd bought some chicks at the feed store a couple of years ago and that rooster had been one of the chicks.

Lucy returned and Essie stopped talking.

"Problem?" Essie asked.

"Not one I can't handle." Lucy slipped the phone back in her pocket. "My business partner, Boone Wilder, has to go into the hospital for a few days. They've got a job in Austin so they're going to need me down there next week."

She glanced at Dane with a worried look that he didn't understand. Was she wondering how he felt about her job or about her leaving?

"What about Maria?" Essie asked.

"Alex is here. Most of the time. And it's just a few days."

Essie muttered to herself, and he thought he heard something about a few days this time, but what about later.

As the two of them discussed Lucy's job, Dane glanced at the garden. A person didn't plant a garden if they weren't committed to staying and seeing it through. Right?

Why should it matter so much to him? He had more than one buyer interested in the ranch. And he'd complicated things by kissing Lucy a second time. The first time he could have written off as an accident.

But today? Yeah, he had definitely meant that kiss.

Chapter Thirteen

When Sunday morning rolled around and Lucy walked out of her room dressed for church, she knew she'd cause a commotion. Maria was at the kitchen table with a bowl of cereal, but when she spotted Lucy in a dress and sandals, she choked a little. She covered it up by pretending to cough.

"Are you going somewhere?" Maria asked as she dipped her spoon into the bowl for another bite of frosted something.

"I'm going to church. So go ahead and say everything you need to say. I want to get it over with."

"Um, one, I've never seen you in a dress. Ever." Maria started with that, actually ticking it off on her finger. "Two, you never go to church. Three, you really dislike church. Four, there is the whole antichurch thing."

"Stop." Lucy stalked past her, intent on getting a bowl of cereal. "Is Alex back in from the barn?"

"Yeah, he's in the shower. And Willa is getting Seth ready for church. She's still avoiding Alex. He makes her nervous."

Lucy poured cereal in her bowl. "Alex makes her nervous?"

"Men are not on her 'favorite things' list right now."

Lucy poured milk over her cereal. "Gotcha. When do we need to leave?"

"Fifteen minutes." Maria put her bowl in the sink and kissed Lucy's cheek. "I'm glad you're going."

"Yeah, me too."

Her heart quaked at the idea. But she refused to let fear control her. She would face it now the same way she'd faced it at other times in her life. She would confront what frightened her. She'd confronted the room in the stable. Each day she walked past it; sometimes she walked in, to show herself that the room wouldn't harm her. It couldn't control her.

Church couldn't harm her. Church was not the enemy. It was a place of charity and compassion, not abuse.

"Are we ready?"

She jumped at the question but she finished her cereal and nodded before facing her brother. He stood at the doorway, his dark hair still damp and curly from the shower.

"I'm ready."

"You okay?"

"Yes, of course I'm okay."

Alex did the unthinkable. He crossed the room and gave her a big hug. "It's okay, sis, we'll be together."

She let him hug her, then she squirmed free. "Go away."

Ten minutes later they pulled into the parking lot of the Bluebonnet Community Church. The parking lot was full. People were talking out front and others were going in through the double doors. It had never been this way when her father pastored the church.

There were seven signs of a cult, she'd read. Opposing critical thinking was at the top of the list. Isolating members came next.

The people in her father's church had either followed blindly or been afraid to speak. He had taken over their thoughts, their families, their lives. He'd been charismatic, as Bea had tried to communicate. They'd seen him as a smiling, engaging speaker who cared about them.

She was slow to get out of the car. As she finally exited and followed Alex, Maria, Willa and Seth, she thought about her father. He hadn't always been mean. He wouldn't have had his following if that had been the case. He'd known how to draw people in.

"Greetings, Palermo family." Pastor Matthews stood at the door of the church. He grabbed Lucy by the hand and didn't let go. He probably feared she would run.

But she wasn't running. Dane had asked her to be here, so here she was. It seemed important. To him. And to her.

"Pastor. Good morning." She made a real attempt at smiling and he released her hand. She walked inside, Alex next to her. Maria came in behind them, with Willa and Seth.

Dane came over to her as she entered. Issy and him. She took a deep breath, finding peace. Because it wasn't the same church her father had pastored. She saw that now. The people were different, save a few familiar faces. The place was lighter, less stern. The pastor wasn't watching them with hawkish awareness, making sure no one transgressed.

And Dane was there with Issy.

"Will you sit with us?" Dane asked as he guided them toward a pew midway up the front of the church. Essie was already there. She waved, but then went back to a conversation with the woman sitting next to her.

"I guess we will."

They all slid into the pew. Willa, her little boy on her lap, Maria, Alex, Lucy, Dane and Issy. As they got situated, Issy moved to Lucy's lap. She looked up with big blue eyes and blond ringlets, her expression sweetly innocent.

"I got a kitten."

"Yes, I heard about that." Lucy dropped a kiss on the child's head. If she focused on Issy, the anxiety couldn't come back for a counterattack. "Did you name it?"

"Lucy."

"You named your kitty Lucy?"

Issy nodded and rested her head on Lucy's shoulder. The musicians moved to the front of the church. A guitarist, a pianist and a fiddle player. They started with a newer song, one that Lucy hadn't heard before.

The rest of the service was a blur. She focused on just being there and making it through that hour of music and a message about faith. She made it through an hour of sitting next to Dane, his arm sometimes drifting to rest across the back of the pew, his hand occasionally touching her arm, rubbing lightly.

As the sermon ended she realized she had survived. There had been no condemnations, no finger-pointing, no beating people up for lack of faith. She had friends who lived their faith in quiet ways that made a difference. Those friends had helped her along the way, opening her eyes to the absolute wrongness of her father's doctrine.

But it had taken time for her to step back inside a

church and reexamine her own faith. Because maybe it was still there, deep inside, scarred and beat up, but living.

They slowly filed out of church, getting stuck in various pockets of people stopping to talk. There was an open, friendly atmosphere. Maria glanced back at her, a "see, I told you" smile on her face. Tight-lipped, Lucy smiled back.

"Are you still taking Willa to her aunt's?" Dane asked as they left the church.

Once they were in a clearing where she could breathe, Lucy answered. "Yes. We've talked about it. She could stay here, but she wants to be as far from Johnny as she can get. She wants to start over and she knows she can't do that if she stays in this area."

"I'll help you move her," he offered.

"You don't have to do that."

"I don't mind. The aunt lives near Austin, right?"

"Yes, but then I'm staying for a few days. I have to work."

"I'll drive back once we have her settled."

Why wasn't he taking no for an answer? She was used to her business partners doing that, but even they knew when to back off. And there was also this trip to church. She was here because he'd asked.

It was on the tip of her tongue to ask him when suddenly a car roared into the parking lot.

"Who is that?" Maria asked, stepping close to Lucy.

"That's Johnny. Willa's husband." Lucy did a quick search for Willa and spotted her a good distance away. "Why didn't County let us know he'd been released?"

Dane handed Issy to Lucy and he hurried in the direction of the car. Lucy gave Issy to her sister. "Go inside. Take Issy and tell people to go back into the sanctuary."

Pastor Matthews appeared, his expression grim. He started moving people toward the church. Lucy sprinted across the parking lot, despite her high heels. Johnny was already out of the car and had hold of Willa. Dane was still a good distance away from them. But he might not have seen what Lucy saw. A knife.

Lucy said a prayer as she kicked off her shoes and circled back behind Willa's husband. She prayed Willa would remember what she'd been taught in the last few days. As Lucy circled them, she made eye contact with Dane, shaking her head and pointing to the knife that Johnny had at his side.

Dane stopped moving and held out an arm to stop others from moving forward. "Hey, Johnny, good to see you."

Johnny didn't seem amused. "Dude, I don't even know you. Back off or I'll cut her."

Willa had Seth by the hand but she let go and told him to run. The little boy obeyed, running for Lucy and hugging her tightly around the waist. She brushed a hand through his hair and told him he was safe and his mommy would be safe. Someone appeared at her side. Pastor Matthews. He lifted the little boy.

"Willa, be calm. Remember." Lucy said it quietly, hoping Johnny wouldn't catch on. Dane kept talking.

Johnny was agitated, his movements jerky. He hadn't been out of jail long but odds were he was already messed up.

Willa must have heard her because she relaxed, just slightly. Johnny loosened his grip, and when he did, Willa spun, bringing her head up under his chin. He jerked back and she brought the palm of her hand up, knocking him backward before bringing her knee up. He fell to the ground and she ran. Dane caught her, holding her tight.

Lucy wanted to cheer but she'd do that later. Instead she ran forward and forced Johnny to the ground, her knee in his back. "And that, Johnny, is how a low-life abuser learns a lesson."

"Get off me, you…"

She pushed his face down. "Ah, ah, ah. Watch your language. We're at church."

"Good job, Lucy." Pastor Matthews knelt next to her. "The police should be here in a minute to give Johnny a ride back to County."

"That's good, because I've worked up an appetite." Lucy grinned at the pastor. "This is a good day."

Because Willa had learned that she had power.

"Yeah, it is a good day. I think we need to add self-defense classes to our lesson plan." Pastor Matthews stepped away as the officer arrived to take custody of Johnny.

As she watched the cop read Johnny his rights, she wondered how it happened that a man could beat his wife to such a degree and spend only days in jail.

"You okay?" Dane appeared at her side.

"Of course I am." His arm went around her and she allowed him to pull her close. Only a fool would deny that gesture of comfort from a man who smelled as good as he looked.

Or maybe only a fool would get this close to a man when she knew that nothing could come of this relationship.

Dane helped Lucy move Willa to her aunt's place, then he and Issy headed home. A Realtor from San

Antonio had called him while they were on the road, telling him she was headed to the ranch with a prospective buyer. He pulled up just as they were getting in the Realtor's SUV.

Dane parked, unlatched Issy and met the real estate agent and the buyers midway across the lawn. He held out a hand to the Realtor, an older woman with deep auburn hair and dark sunglasses that kept him from seeing her eyes. Not particularly a look that endeared him to her.

"Mr. Scott, good to meet you. I'm Liza McMillan. The Andersons really enjoyed your property."

He managed a smile. "Thank you."

It didn't come out sounding a bit harsh. Or so he told himself as he stood there smiling at the couple, who didn't look as if they knew the front of an Angus from the back. But they did have nice boots.

The front door of the house closed with a definite thud. He glanced back and saw Haven heading his way. To the rescue. She was good at rescuing everyone but herself.

"Dane, did you meet the Andersons?" She forced a smile that wasn't much more genuine than his.

What in the world was he doing? This ranch had been in his family for over one hundred years. His great-grandparents had held on to the land during the Depression. His parents had farmed it until his dad's health forced him to call it quits. And Dane was going to give it up?

Haven touched his arm and smiled up at him, reassuring and sweet. "Let me take Issy in the house."

He handed his daughter over, giving her a last hug. She patted Haven's cheek. That was Issy's way of familiarizing herself with people. She couldn't look in their eyes, see their smile or expression, but she could pat their face, kiss their cheek and know their mood with a touch.

As they walked away he heard his daughter whisper, "Daddy's upset."

The Realtor, Liza, watched his daughter leave, then her attention was on him. Big questions loomed in her eyes as she pulled off those dark designer sunglasses.

"Mr. Scott, I was informed you want to sell because you need to relocate to Dallas for your daughter's schooling."

He stood there a long minute, letting his gaze wander over the property, the cattle, the barns and horses. For his daughter.

"You're correct."

"Okay, I just wanted to make sure." She glanced back at the couple, who had taken a seat in her SUV. "I think we'll have an offer for you in a day or two."

He swallowed regret and nodded. "Sounds good."

She left. He watched the dust swirl behind her vehicle until she turned onto the highway blacktop, and then he headed for the barn. What he needed right now was to clear his head. As he walked, he whistled.

By the time he got to the stable, his horse, Daniel, was at the fence. The big bay, red with dark legs and a black mane and tail, looked ready for a ride. Dane pulled a saddle and bridle out of the tack room and went back for a halter and lead.

Daniel was waiting for him. He brought the horse in, cross tied him in the center aisle and saddled him. He knew that Haven would understand. She would feed Issy. They would watch cartoons.

He didn't know what he'd do without his sister. But

he also knew that she needed to live her own life. And it was time for him to move on with his.

He put his left foot in the stirrup and swung his leg over the saddle. Daniel shuffled about a bit but then he was ready to go. As he rode off, Dane looked back at the stone-and-stucco ranch house, built by his parents after the old wooden house burned down when Dane had been a toddler. It was a good house. His mom had designed it. His dad had built it from the foundation up.

When he'd sat them down to tell them about putting the ranch on the market, they hadn't balked. They knew he needed to put Issy first. Whatever was best for his child, they'd said. It had set his mind at ease, somewhat.

Daniel picked his way along the trail and Dane eased into the ride. The horse knew this path well and as the ground smoothed out and as Dane loosened his hold on the reins, the horse eased into a canter.

It had been a summer day when he'd ridden along this fence trail and spotted Lucy coming up from the creek. He'd watched from a distance as she'd dismounted and led her big palomino to the shade of a tree. She'd sprawled out on the grass with a book. The horse had grazed a short distance away.

This spot had been her escape. Her hiding place. It was Scott land so her father wouldn't come on the property. He never found the spot in the fence where she'd sneaked through.

As he drew closer to the creek he never expected to see her on this day the same as he had then. But with the sun low on the horizon he saw the movement of a horse in the trees along the edge of the creek. He pulled Daniel back and the horse slowed, and then stopped. Even from that distance he knew that it was Lucy. He gave his horse a nudge forward. Daniel broke into a trot and whinnied a greeting to the other horse.

The chestnut mare Alex had bought returned the greeting, shaking her fine head. The rider walked out of the woods, spotted him and paused. Dane rode on, not at all put off by her appearance. She might not have wanted company but she wouldn't send him away.

What would he say to her? It would keep things simple if he waved and rode off, leaving her to read or doze in the grass, whatever she had planned. Stopping would definitely complicate things between them. Neither of them needed complications.

"Looks like we had the same idea," Lucy said as he approached and dismounted.

"Seemed like a good way to unwind." He led his horse closer and noticed that her hair was wet. "You took a swim?"

She raised her hand to her hair, a self-conscious gesture. "No, just splashed my face and hair. It felt good. It's been a long time since I've been down here."

"Twelve years." He thought it should feel different after twelve years, but it didn't. It felt frighteningly similar, as if he was still a kid discovering something beautiful on the shores of this creek.

He wondered how no one else had ever noticed her. Why was she still single and wary?

"Yes," she said. "Twelve years."

There was a long pause, then she shook her head, as if clearing her thoughts. "We're no longer those two kids anymore."

"True."

"I'm not sure what we're doing here, Dane."

He laughed. "Probably the same thing. We must have both needed a ride on a summer day to clear our heads?"

"You know that isn't what I meant. Us. We can't go back to being those two kids."

"No, we can't. I have a daughter now."

"And I have more baggage than any man should have to deal with."

And that's where their opinions differed. Because he didn't see her as a woman with baggage. He saw her as a woman with layers. And those layers made her unique, strong, determined.

"I guess we both have baggage," he said as he narrowed the distance between them. "But I refuse to see my daughter as baggage. She's the best thing I've ever done."

"I agree." Her voice was a little bit breathless. And then she surprised him by touching his face, her fingers lingering.

"I don't know how to walk away, Lucy. I don't know how to not be impressed by you, drawn to you."

"We're too old for a summer romance," she warned.

"I know."

He kissed her, his lips moving over hers as she continued touching his cheek, her hand eventually moving to the back of his neck. He never wanted summer to end if this was a summer romance.

As the kiss ended, she rested her cheek against his. He felt the dampness of her hair against his face and felt her eyelashes graze his skin as she closed her eyes. He held her close and wondered how often she allowed herself to be held. He wondered how he could ever let her go.

"Summer romances stink," she whispered.

"It doesn't have to be just a summer romance." The words were out and he couldn't take them back. But he had no right to make promises.

He'd be a fool to promise anything. But he'd be an even-bigger fool to let her go because since she'd driven back into his life, he felt whole. He hadn't felt whole in a long time.

"It is a summer romance." She kissed his cheek and stepped away. "And I'm too old for games. I'm single, set in my ways, and I don't want to hurt you or Issy. I can't give you false hope."

"What is it that makes you believe you can't be the person we want in our lives?"

"Fear," she said simply. "I'm afraid. Of being controlled. I'm afraid I'll feel trapped or that I'll give up my power."

"I would never hurt you, Lucy."

She nodded but he got the feeling she didn't believe him.

"What brought you out here today, Dane?"

He touched his forehead to hers. "More people looking to buy the ranch."

She smiled so sweetly, her brown eyes melting to chocolate. "You have the power to hurt me, you know. I think I'm more afraid of you than I've ever been of anyone in my whole life."

That shook him to the core because he knew the abuse she'd suffered. How could he be the person she most feared?

She smiled up at him. "You don't get it, do you?"

"No, I guess I don't."

"I've never wanted to give up my power to anyone the way I want to give it up to you."

She walked away, a woman unwilling to give up control of her life. And he understood. She came from a place where power and control meant everything negative.

For her, control meant freedom and strength. Of course she wouldn't give those things up. Not to anyone.

How could he convince her that she could give herself to someone without giving up who she was? He didn't want to take from her. He'd realized something in the last few weeks. Having the right person at his side made him stronger.

Maybe she did realize that and it frightened her. Perhaps it should frighten him, too.

Chapter Fourteen

Lucy walked the perimeter of the hotel conference area, Daron McKay at her side. He was a fellow soldier, a friend and her business partner. They'd shared almost everything. She'd known when he was falling in love with his wife, Emma. She'd known when he had nightmares stemming from Afghanistan.

But she didn't know how to share with him that she was in over her head with Dane Scott. Even after spending the last couple of days working in Austin with him, she still couldn't put it into words.

"You're quiet today." Daron made the observation as they studied the exits from the room. "Anything I need to know about?"

She wanted to shrug it off but she couldn't. He was the closest thing she had to a best friend. "My little sister is having a baby."

"Yeah, you said that when you called." He checked the lock and the alarms on the door. "Boone and I will take care of things and you take care of your family. Pregnancy is only nine months, not forever."

"Right," she mumbled as they kept moving. What was she supposed to tell him, that her sister was the least of her worries? That sounded heartless. Instead she was very worried about her sister, about the baby that Maria wasn't sure she would keep.

"This isn't about your sister, is it?" Daron took off his cowboy hat and smoothed back his hair.

"Not really. It's about…" She kept walking but not before she saw the amused glint in his eyes. "Just leave me alone."

He caught up with her, laughing. "Has Lucy Palermo fallen for a man?"

"Shut up, jerk." She kept walking, picking up speed and hoping he would just go away. He wouldn't, though.

"Come on, Luce, you're human. You are actually a decent human being." He made a face. "Okay, I'm only going to say this once because we're friends and in a weird way you've always been one of the guys. You're a girl, but you've just been our friend. We forget that you're a woman."

"Thanks. That's so reassuring. I'm one of the guys."

"This is awkward. Like giving Boone advice."

"Again, not really helping." She put a hand on her holstered gun.

The gesture broke the awkwardness of the moment and Daron laughed. "Okay, let me be honest. You're difficult to get to know. Your attitude puts people off and sometimes frightens small children."

She stopped him. "Small children like me. Your daughter loves me."

Issy loved her, too. And she thought Dane's little girl was the best thing ever. But when Dane had asked her to go to church, it had felt as if he were testing her.

She got it; a couple shouldn't be unequally yoked. It made sense. A couple should have common ground because if they didn't, the ground would always be shifting beneath them.

"My daughter does love you," Daron said simply. "Children and animals see the real you. Emma and I love you. Boone and Kayla love you. Our families love you. Yes, you do your best to push us all away. But the truth is, Lucy, you're one of the best people I know. When Emma needed you, you were there for her. For us."

His words warmed her cheeks and she had to move away so that he wouldn't see that his speech had brought tears to her eyes. The man could be so ruthless when he was being kind. She would have gotten away from him but he tugged her back and into his big, stupid arms. She squeezed her eyes shut and remained stiff as he held her close and patted her back.

"I'm not a child who skinned her knee," she blubbered against his shoulder. "And I don't cry."

"No, you're a woman who hasn't figured out that there are people worth trusting." He let out a pained sigh. "Lucy, you're beautiful."

She pulled out of his embrace and wiped at her eyes. "I can't believe you made me cry. It wasn't that long ago that you were watching Emma from a distance, pretending you weren't desperately in love with her."

"I can now admit that I was but a shell of a man without her."

Lucy rolled her eyes. "I'm done getting in touch with my inner self or inner child or whatever it is you think I need to do. I'm fine. Really." She stomped off.

"Of course you are." He caught up with her as they exited the conference room. "Lucy, if this guy is the one, give him a chance."

They made their way to the bank of elevators and

Daron pushed the up button. "I know that I like him. That doesn't make him The One. I like you and I would never think of us as a couple." She shuddered.

"That's because I'm not The One."

They stepped into the elevator and he pushed the button for the floor where their client waited. Lucy waited until the other occupants stepped off the elevator before she resumed their conversation.

"I've spent a lot of my life avoiding relationships," she admitted. "I'm afraid. I don't know how to open up and I don't want to lose myself to a person who might let me down."

The elevator doors started to open. Daron pushed the button to close them. "I think what you want to say is that you're afraid you'll marry a man like your father and you won't know it until it's too late. I would advise you to trust yourself. Because if you don't, you're going to spend your entire life avoiding what might be the best thing that ever happened to you. We all have stuff we've gone through, Lucy. So you say you don't want a man to have control of you, but you're letting your father control every single day of your life. Every time you shut yourself off, he's controlling you."

The doors opened and they stepped onto the tenth floor.

"Thank you. For the advice," Lucy said.

"You're welcome. I only hope that you take it." He led her to the door at the end of the hall where their client waited for them.

Then it was time to work. Their client was notorious for avoiding his security detail. That's why the two of them weren't trusting this project to the men they sometimes contracted to help with bigger jobs.

She loved her work. She'd spent the last few years

building a business that she'd never planned to walk away from. It was going to be her life, this business. For years the ranch had been an afterthought, the place she least wanted to be. Her family had become strangers to her.

That call from Aunt Essie a month ago had changed everything.

When she opened the door to her apartment in Austin she knew something wasn't right. She stood in the hall and withdrew her gun from the holster. With cautious steps she peered through the opening, and then she stepped inside. The lights were on. The television was blaring. Something was burning.

She stepped into the kitchen, where a pan had been left on the burner. Something black and fried beyond recognition sizzled in the pan. She turned it off and walked through the apartment. She went room to room, checking closets, under furniture, behind curtains.

The apartment was empty. But she wasn't imagining that someone had been there. Someone had left the pan on the stove. Someone had turned on lights. But who?

Lucy dialed her phone. Because she needed a friend, and in the last few weeks she'd realized she had few people in her life that fit that role. She needed to talk this out with someone.

A month ago she would have called Daron or Boone. But things had changed. In the past year they'd married and weren't as accessible as they used to be. And tonight the first person she thought of was Dane.

"Hey, neighbor." Dane's voice was strong and familiar, and as soon as she heard it, she cried.

Dane drove over to the Palermo ranch the next morning. He and Lucy had talked for almost two hours the previous evening. He'd stayed on the phone with her as she drove home. She'd finished the job in Austin, and she said she just wanted to get back to Bluebonnet.

Last night she'd sounded like someone who really needed another person to lean on. He didn't know how she'd feel in the light of day.

"Daddy, is Lucy home?" Issy asked as he parked the truck.

"Yes, she's home." He spotted her in the arena. She was working the grullo horse from the Murrays. When she decided to do something, she didn't waste time. She must have gone and bought the horse that morning.

He helped Issy out of her car seat and she pushed at him a little when he tried to lift her into his arms.

"I can do it," she said. She wanted to walk. Apparently she didn't want to be carried through life. He got it. It wasn't easy but he could let go.

"I know you can do it, honey." He put her down and held her hand.

She stopped, cocking her head to listen. "Where is Lucy?"

"She's riding a horse in the arena."

"A big horse?" she asked with such a hopeful tone that he knew she wondered if Lucy might have the pony out.

"Yes, a big horse."

She sighed and tilted her head down, dejected.

"I'll see if she can bring Cobalt out for you to pet," he offered.

Her face brightened, and she nodded as she hurried along at his side.

Lucy saw them coming. She eased back on the reins and spoke to the horse. The animal, the softest gray with a hint of brown, slowed its pace. With minimal use of reins, she turned the horse toward the stable.

"Hey, you two," she called out as she slid to the ground in a graceful, fluid motion.

"Daddy said you might get the pony out." Issy tugged on his hand and he raised his gaze to meet Lucy's.

"Did he? Well, it just so happens that little pony is in the back corral and really wishing he could spend time with someone. But before we do that, would you like to ride Lolly here?"

"I don't know," Dane said, because his daughter on a horse might be more than his heart could take.

"Trust me," Lucy said softly with a hint of a smile on her face.

He wanted to say the same. But maybe that phone call last night had been a first step.

She waited for him to make the decision. He nodded and she scooped his daughter up, making her giggle. He remained silent, although he desperately wanted to tell her to be careful. Instead he moved to the fence, where he could watch them.

"I'm going to put you on first," Lucy told his daughter. "Hold on."

She put Issy's hands on the pommel of the saddle. The mare didn't move. She didn't flinch. With attentive ears she waited for her new owner's command.

Lucy put her left foot in the stirrup and swung her right leg over the mare's back. She settled behind Issy and wrapped her arms around his daughter. And then she put the reins in Issy's hands. Dane moved to the gate. He watched as the horse and riders made a lap around the arena. When they picked up speed, he heard his daughter's giggles and watched her turn in the saddle to tell Lucy something that made them both laugh.

The ride lasted only a few minutes.

"That wasn't so bad, was it?" Lucy asked him, not his daughter.

"No, not so bad."

"She's going to help me brush Lolly, and then we'll get Cobalt. Unless you want to get the pony while we take care of Lolly?"

"I'll get the pony." He watched as the two of them led the big mare to the stable. After they were out of sight he headed for the back corral, where Cobalt was busy rolling in thick grass. He whistled and the pony came to his feet, shook himself from head to tail, then trotted to the fence.

When he led the pony into the stable, Lucy was putting her new mare back into a stall. Maria had joined them. She rested her hand on her belly and knelt down to talk to Issy. The three of them looked up when he approached with the pony.

"Hey, it's Cobalt," Maria called out. Issy clapped her hands at the announcement.

"Let me get his bridle and saddle," Lucy said as she opened the tack room door. But Dane saw her gaze slide to that room she'd left empty, even though she'd removed the boards that she'd hammered over the entrance.

"After Issy rides Cobalt, can she come to the house with me?" Maria asked. "I'm making cookies."

"Can I, Daddy?" She reached for Maria. "Chocolate chip?"

"Yes, chocolate chip," Maria answered as she took a seat on an overturned bucket. She grimaced as she sat down and he wondered if she was okay. He would mention it to Lucy. Because someone needed to watch over her.

"Daddy, chocolate chip!" She reminded him that she still needed an answer.

"Yes, Issy, you may go with Maria."

A few minutes later she forgot all about chocolate chip cookies as she straddled Cobalt and Lucy handed her the reins. He followed along behind them as Lucy taught his daughter how to ride the pony. He wanted to remind her that Isabelle wasn't yet four. She was his only child. She couldn't see.

But Issy was giggling and Lucy appeared carefree. Maybe they both needed this moment. One of them needed to be a child and the other needed to let go and not worry.

They made their way over to the arena. Maria didn't follow; she said she was happy sitting on that bucket. She would wait for them there.

"Lucy, can we go fast?" Issy asked, trying to use the reins to encourage the pony to a faster pace. She had ridden with him a few times. And she'd paid attention.

"No, we can't run fast." He and Lucy answered the same thing at the same time.

"Okay, no running." Issy sighed; the sound couldn't have been more pathetic. She wanted her disappointment to be obvious.

"But you're riding your very own pony," Lucy reminded her as they walked along the edge of the arena.

"My very own?" Issy asked.

Lucy avoided looking his way and she didn't answer his daughter. But he should have known.

"Do you want to feel him trot?" Lucy asked to distract her, he was sure.

"Yes, please."

She led the pony back toward the stable and the plucky little animal gave them his best trot. Lucy held tight to Issy, talking to her the entire time. Dane stood at the gate. His daughter was having fun and she was safe. He was letting go. But it wasn't easy.

When they got back to the stable, he helped his daughter off the pony. A wide grin lit up her little face and she hugged him with all her might. She'd ridden her first pony. And Maria was waiting to take her to make chocolate chip cookies.

Life at this moment was good.

After Issy left with Maria, he gave Lucy his full attention. She was busy brushing the pony, pretending it was natural that she'd come home in the middle of the night, that they'd talked the whole drive home, and that at times she'd been tearful.

"What happened?" he asked. It had to be something major because Lucy had called him. She'd been crying.

She shook her head as she unhooked the pony's lead rope from the rings on the side of the stable.

"Someone was in my apartment."

She hadn't said a word about it the previous evening. She'd only told him she needed to talk.

"Who?"

"I don't know. They left lights on and put a pan on the stove. I'm assuming they wanted me to know they'd been there."

He put a hand on her shoulder and she flinched beneath his touch. Her gaze lingered on that room. He wondered if the intruder had something to do with her past.

He leaned to kiss her cheek from behind. She leaned back against him, her head tucked safely under his chin. For several minutes they stood like that in the quiet of the stable. Rain started to fall and a breeze blew through. Lucy shivered and he held her a little closer.

"I came home because I didn't know what to do," she finally said.

"About the person in your apartment?"

"About that and other things." She sighed, a soft sound that vibrated through him. "About the ranch. About Maria. About us. I always know what to do."

So there was an "us." He had started to think so. But he was as confused as she was. He knew who he was without her. He didn't know who he was with her. Or to her.

"Us." He let the word slip out in the silence of the stable. She nodded, although her back was to him and her head was still tucked beneath his chin.

"I never saw myself as part of an 'us.'" She said it as if it was her last confession. "I still have trouble being a part of this, of us. I'm standing here in your arms and it feels so right. But it feels so scary, too. Like you could just take hold…"

He kissed the top of her head. "I'll never hurt you, Lucy. Never," he said.

"But you might. Because what happens when I go back to work. What happens when you sell the ranch? There are so many unknowns. What if I can't be the person who stays in one place, and who's happy being a wife and mother?"

Ah, now she was tapping into all his fears.

"I don't know," he admitted.

She was right; he could hurt her. She could hurt him, too. They could hurt Issy.

But first things first—they had to figure out who had been in her apartment.

Chapter Fifteen

A week later Maria reminded her that she had a doctor's appointment. They arrived early, checked in with the receptionist, and then sat down to wait.

"I'm sorry that you have to stay in Bluebonnet," Maria said as they waited.

Lucy looked up from the magazine she'd been flipping through. "Is that what you think? I'm not sorry, Maria."

"I don't know what to think anymore," Maria said, her gaze focused on the window and the parking lot. "I know you have a lot of reasons why you don't want to be here. Why you'd rather be in Austin. I know you don't want to stay."

"It isn't that simple," Lucy told her sister, setting the magazine back on the table. "I will admit that I hadn't thought about coming home. I have a business and friends in Austin. But I have family here. *You* are my family."

"What about Dane?" her sister asked with a hint of humor flashing in her toffee-colored eyes.

"Dane is a friend. That's all."

"Right, okay. A friend that you're constantly with.

His daughter loves you. The two of you are working together at the shelter."

"I'd rather not discuss this," she said, shaking her head. "There isn't a relationship. We're friends."

The receptionist called Maria's name and saved Lucy from further discussion. She followed her sister back to the exam room, where a nurse explained that they would be doing the ultrasound. She explained the procedure and Maria nodded the entire time, her face lighting up as she took in the magnitude of this moment.

As she stretched out on the exam table for the ultrasound, Maria reached for Lucy's hand. "Today this bump becomes somebody. A little boy or a little girl."

"I know." Maria focused on the screen as the technician started the ultrasound. "It has a face and hands. And feet. It's a tiny person."

Lucy was nearly speechless as a little person came into view on the screen. A tiny face. Tiny fingers.

"It's a girl," the technician announced with a smile.

Maria looked at Lucy. "I told you."

Maria squeezed her little sister's hand. "Yes, you did."

"Raise her for me," Maria whispered. "Be her mom, Lucy. You'll be a good mom. I'm still a kid. I can't do this."

"I'll be here for you."

Maria shook her head. "No, you won't. But I want you to be there for her."

"Maria, we'll talk about this later."

The technician gave them a soft and sympathetic smile as she turned off the machine and told Maria she was all done. Maria sat up, visibly doing her best to pull herself together. She wiped her face with a tissue the nurse had given her and then she hopped down from the exam table. Without a look back, she walked out of the room.

Lucy let her go, giving her a few minutes to calm down. When she came into the waiting room, she discovered that Maria was already outside. She was sitting on a bench at the front of the building, the tissue still in her hand. Lucy sat down next to her.

"I don't know what to do," Maria told her.

"I know. I'm sorry for doing that to you. It wasn't fair. None of this is fair. Not really. You planned on going to college to be a doctor. I planned on building up my business. We both made choices because we had to do what was best for other people. I am here for you. You're having this baby because you're giving her a life. And the rest will work itself out."

"Right, of course it will. But when it's all said and done, where will this journey take us? All because of one really stupid mistake on my part. I'm changing all of our lives because I messed up."

"You didn't mess up, Maria. Look at it this way—the two of us have gotten closer. I've learned that church isn't all bad. You have adults you can turn to for help."

"Thank you," Maria said, leaning against her. "I'm glad we've gotten to know each other better. And I'm glad this bump is a girl." She touched her stomach.

"Stop it." Lucy laughed as she got up and pulled her sister to her feet. "You have to give her a name."

Maria shook her head. "No, I don't want to do that. I don't want to name her, and then have to give her up."

"You're serious about giving her up?"

"I am," Maria said with conviction. "I've made mistakes but giving her up is not a mistake. It's one thing that feels right. I've prayed about it, Lucy. I've made peace with this decision."

"You know I'll support you whatever you decide to do." Lucy opened her truck door and waited for Maria to get in. "I want you to know, I'm proud of you."

Maria laughed. "Thanks. I'm proud of me, too. Let's get this show on the road. I'm starving and the only thing that sounds good is that fruit dip you made last night. I can't get enough of that stuff."

"Must be the pregnancy."

"I guess. But at least it's healthy."

Lucy shook her head at that. "Fruit dip being healthy is debatable."

They were just a few miles out of Bluebonnet when Lucy's phone rang. She saw Dane's name on the caller ID.

"Hey, what's up?" She motioned to her sister to turn down the radio. It had been a fight to and from the doctor's office. Maria liked pop music. Lucy was country all the way.

"Are you all on your way home?"

"Yes. Why?" She hesitated to ask. "What's happened?"

"There's been a fire."

"A fire?"

"At the church. They put it out before it could do any major damage."

"Any clues as to who did it?"

"None. But whoever it was, they knew the code and deactivated the security system."

"We have a list of people who have that code," Lucy said.

"Yes, they're questioning people now."

"I'll be there in twenty minutes."

"Be careful. And, Lucy, I think you should tell the

police about the break-in at your apartment. It doesn't feel like a coincidence."

She agreed. "You're right. And there have been other incidents that I've ignored. We'll talk when I get back to town."

How had she not seen this? She provided security for a living and she had ignored the signs. She'd ignored the boards ripped off that room. She'd ignored that someone had been in the house.

No more ignoring.

"Do you know who did it?" Maria asked.

"I don't have a clue." She focused on the road and shook her head. "That isn't true. There is a clue. It's someone with the code. Someone from the church."

"From the Community Church? That doesn't make sense."

"No, someone from the Church of the Redeemed. Someone angry either with our father or that Jesse Palermo's church, his legacy, is being torn apart and rebuilt into something good."

"I don't think our father had many fans."

"No, but there were a few." She shot her sister a concerned look. "Until we figure this out, I want you to be careful. When you're in the house alone, I want the doors locked."

"You're making me nervous."

"I know and I'm sorry. But I want you safe."

Lucy slowed to pull into the church parking lot. The fire truck was still on scene. The police were standing next to the building talking.

"Wow, life is never boring in a small town," Maria said.

"Isn't that the truth," Lucy agreed. She parked next to Dane's truck. "Do you want to stay here?"

Maria shook her head. "No, I think I'd rather go with you."

As they walked up the sidewalk, Dane joined them. "The system was definitely turned off by someone who knew the code. They're talking to Pastor Matthews, his wife, Elaine and a few others."

"None of them would want to see this ministry hurt." It didn't make sense. Whoever this was, they wanted to send a message.

"Do you think it was a spouse of one of the women?" Maria asked.

"It's possible." Lucy headed around the side of the building. She'd just been here the day before, giving the women their first lesson in self-defense. "I know it looks minor, but can it be fixed?"

"Yes, the fire truck got here within minutes. If it had been at night, it might have been a different story."

"Can I go inside?" Maria asked.

Lucy looked to Dane. He nodded. "The sanctuary is clear. You can sit in there if you want."

He watched Maria walk away, waiting until she was out of earshot before he spoke again. "Is she okay?"

Lucy realized that he would worry, because Issy had been born early. "She's fine, just tired. She's having a little girl, by the way."

A grin split across his handsome face at the news. "Another little girl to wrap us all around her little fingers."

"She wants to give her up for adoption." Lucy brushed a hand over her eyes. "She asked me to raise her."

"And?"

"And I told her I wasn't sure I could do that. I understand she wants to do what's best for the baby and she feels as if she isn't ready to be a mom. But I'm not sure if I'm the right person for the job."

"You have time to think it over."

She spotted Pastor Matthews coming around the corner. He looked beaten down but still managed a half smile.

"Have either of you seen Elaine? They want to talk to her."

Dane shook his head. "I got here after the fire truck and first responders. She wasn't here."

Pastor Matthews scratched his chin. "I don't know that she was here today. She usually helps out in the kitchen and the nursery. I'll call her again. Maybe she's out of town."

Maybe, Lucy thought. But she doubted it. She remembered Elaine's husband, a man who had followed Jesse Palermo without question.

She looked up and Dane was studying her, his blue eyes clear and steady.

"We should go check on her," Dane suggested before she could get the words out.

"Yes, we should."

They didn't find Elaine at her house. Dane had worried they wouldn't. They did find signs of a fight. There were broken dishes on the floor, and a broken front door. The police were going to follow up, calling Elaine's family and putting out a BOLO for her and her ex-husband, Jerry.

"Are you and Maria going to be okay tonight?" he asked as he said goodbye to Lucy at her truck.

She grinned and he shook his head.

"You're right, silly question," he admitted.

"But sweet of you to ask."

"Yes, sweet." He brushed a hand through his hair and took a step back from her. "I have to leave now because I want to kiss you good-night."

In response she reached for the truck door. "And we both know that's a bad idea. Dane, we have to step back from this, whatever this is."

"You're right," he admitted. "We both have a lot going on."

He could admit she was right, but all the way home he was thinking that he wanted her to tell him he was wrong. Wanted her to make this easy on him. If she picked him, it might change everything.

He walked through his front door, exhausted. Haven eyed him from her chair in the living room. Issy was curled up asleep on her lap.

He kicked off his boots and walked into the living room, dropping his hat on the coffee table before he stretched out on the sofa. The kitten hurried across the room to curl up with him, because it obviously didn't have a clue about his aversion to cats.

"How's it going?" Haven asked in a hushed tone as she stroked his daughter's curly blond hair.

"Wonderful. How is it possible that when I made a decision a few months ago it felt right, and now it seems completely wrong?"

His sister laughed. "I think sometimes we convince ourselves the wrong answer is the right one because we feel it will make everything better. But then the right answers roll over us, forcing us to let go of our plans and choose God's."

"That didn't help."

"Is this about the offer on the ranch?" she asked quietly, soothingly, as if she was talking to his daughter and not to him.

"The offer on the ranch. Lucy. My own stubborn convictions."

"I'd love to give you advice, but I'm about the worst person to ask."

He sat up so that he could face her, because tonight his little sister sounded as if she might be in a bad place.

"Are you okay?"

She looked down at Issy, sleeping in her arms, and a tear rolled down her cheek. "I've been better."

"I'm sorry, Haven. Is there anything I can do?"

"Undo the past?" She offered a watery, hopeful smile.

"I would if I could."

She sniffed and he pulled a tissue from the box on the table and handed it to her.

"You could do me a favor," she said after a few minutes.

"Name it."

Another grin, this one a little mischievous. "Be happy. And if that means selling the ranch, sell it. If it means keeping it and pursuing a relationship with Lucy, then take the chance and go for it."

"I think Lucy needs space."

"Oh."

He was in love. He had come to that realization as he'd stood in the church parking lot watching Lucy drive away. He hadn't wanted her to go. He wanted to chase her down and tell her that he loved her. He shook his head at the thought. Man, he needed her the way he needed air to breathe. Only problem was, she didn't seem to need anyone.

He wasn't going to do this again. He wasn't going to love a woman who wanted the opposite of everything he wanted. He wanted a marriage that lasted this time.

Not a relationship built on maybes.

"You're making me look like an optimist," Haven whispered.

He glanced at his auburn-haired sister and thought of her heartache, her loss. He felt foolish.

"Don't get that look on your face," she warned him.

"Okay, no looks on my face. Just brotherly concern."

She smiled down at the little girl in her arms. "Issy makes everything better. Do you want to hold her?"

"I will when you're done." He was content to sit and watch Issy sleep. "I think before I take the offer on the ranch, I'll talk to a couple of local schools. If there is one outside our district but close by that might be better for her, I could pay the tuition."

Haven's eyes widened. "That's a big step."

"Yes, it is."

Issy stirred in Haven's arms but went back to sleep as Haven rocked back and forth. "I'm praying for you, Dane. I know this is tough. I know you don't want to give up the ranch. I know you can do your electrical contract work anywhere. But this has been home for a long time."

"I know it has. I promise you, I won't take this offer if it doesn't feel right."

Suddenly his phone rang. "Lucy? Everything okay?"

"They found Elaine in her car on a side road. She was in pretty bad shape. They're calling for medevac and they'll fly her to Austin."

"You'll keep me updated?" he asked, aware that his sister was watching with obvious interest.

"Yes, of course." She paused. "Dane, Maria and I are going to drive up there. We'll stay at my place. Alex will stay here and take care of the ranch. I want to make sure Elaine is okay and I really need to help with the business. One of my partners is injured and needs to be off his feet for at least two weeks. Maybe longer."

For some reason, that sounded like goodbye to him. "If you need anything…"

"I'll call you if I need you," she replied. "Good night."

The call ended.

"What happened?" Haven asked as he hung up.

"They found Elaine Collins. She's in pretty bad shape. Looks like her husband, Jerry, beat her up."

"Why?"

"I'm not really sure. I have a feeling he also broke into Lucy's apartment. Maybe anger over the past, and over doing something different with the church."

"That's really just crazy. Dane, if you want to go check on Lucy, I'll take care of Issy."

"I know you would, but I don't think Lucy wants me there."

"So you'll just give up?"

"It isn't giving up." A better word was accepting reality. Lucy was running scared.

He had received an offer on the ranch that no sane man would turn down.

A month ago the two of them had been living separate lives with separate goals. Maybe this was how they got back on track and remembered those plans.

Or maybe this was how he learned the hard way that he didn't want to be alone anymore.

Chapter Sixteen

Lucy and Maria arrived at the hospital in Austin early the next morning. They took the elevator to the fourth floor, where they found Elaine's room. Lucy knocked softly, waited for an invitation to come in, then pushed the door open.

Maria, looking a little pale, pointed to the waiting room. "I'm going to sit down and wait."

"Are you okay?"

"Just a little icky, but I'll be fine."

Lucy hesitated to leave her alone. "If you need me, I'll be here."

"I know."

Lucy waited until her sister entered the waiting room before she walked into Elaine's room. She smiled at the woman sitting next to the bed. She hadn't seen her in years, but she knew she must be Elaine's mom, Nadine.

"Lucy, how are you?" Elaine asked, her voice hoarse.

"I'm obviously better than you are. Elaine, I'm so sorry."

Elaine's brows drew together. "You aren't to blame."

"Maybe not, but I feel responsible. I wish I'd known."

"That Jerry is a crazy person?" She laughed a little.

"He's obsessed, even after all of these years. He wanted to rebuild the church. He thought if you came back, you'd do it. Because you're a Palermo."

"I'm sorry to disappoint him."

Elaine pointed to the empty chair on the opposite side of her bed. "He was disappointed. So he set out to put you in your place."

"I have news for him. I'm not good at being controlled. But the police got him?"

Elaine's eyes widened. "No, they didn't."

Lucy hadn't known that. The call she'd gotten... The speaker said he'd been caught. But he wasn't in jail. Why wasn't someone here guarding Elaine?

"Elaine, there should be guards at your door."

"I'm not worried, Lucy."

Not worried? About a man who tried to burn the church. A who had beaten her and put her in the hospital. "But you should be worried. And the police should be worried."

Elaine smiled, peaceful, not at all troubled. "He's not going to hurt you."

Lucy shook her head. "What?"

"He just wants you to take your rightful place."

"My rightful place?"

The older woman smiled gently at Lucy, as if she was a child who didn't understand. "Honey, your father always said you would take the pulpit if anything happened to him."

Lucy stood. She had to get out of here. She had to make sure Maria was safe. "You're right. I should have taken my rightful place. If he'd told me, I would have."

"Of course you would have." Elaine reached for her hand. "That's why we had to stop Pastor Matthews from taking over the church. Unfortunately the fire didn't take. But now that you understand, we can work together."

What person in their right mind would ever want to recreate the church that Jesse Palermo had formed? Lucy felt sympathy for Elaine, because the woman didn't understand freedom.

"I should go find Jerry," Lucy said with a smile she had to force. "We'll work things out."

"I'm so glad. We've been having meetings at the Ledbetters', but they're tired of having it in their home."

"Of course they are," Lucy answered as she backed toward the door. "Is Jerry here?"

"In the waiting room," Elaine answered, her eyes closing. "He had to do this, Lucy. I wanted out. I'm sorry."

Her mother told her to hush. Lucy felt a chill sweep up her spine as she looked from mother to daughter. Elaine had wanted out. That was the reason for the beating Jerry had given her. And at the moment he was possibly with her sister.

Lucy rushed down the hall to the waiting room. Jerry sat there, next to Maria. Her sister shot Lucy a worried look and tears formed in her eyes. Her knees were drawn up and her hand was on her belly. She looked young and frightened. She was a girl who needed her mom, but their mother had never been who they needed.

"Jerry, I heard you've been looking for me." Lucy smiled, hoping to appease the man who sat next to her sister. It would be a very bad day for him if he harmed one hair on Maria's head.

"I have been, but I think I changed my mind. Maybe you're weak. Your dad worried about that."

"He shouldn't have worried. I'm not weak."

Jerry squeezed Maria's arm. "Your sister is weak,

too. The minute Matthews showed up in town, Maria and Essie were right there to welcome him. I killed that rooster thinking Essie would get the hint."

"You jerk." Maria spoke with venom in her tone. He reached for her, possibly to quiet her. But Maria had been paying attention. As he reached, her arm shot up. Her palm connected with his chin, knocking his head back. She stood, stomping his toe and giving him a second hit.

"I'm not going to let you get away with that, Maria." Jerry stood, as if he intended to go after her sister. Lucy moved, ready to do whatever she must to keep Maria safe. Jerry backed off, proving he had a bit more sense than she would have guessed.

The door opened, and a police officer stepped into the room, asking if everyone was okay.

"We're fine. Jerry just has a few things he needs to discuss." Lucy grinned at Jerry. "With a judge. Sorry, Jerry, I called 911 before I got down here to talk to you."

"Lucy." Maria's voice sounded as if it came from far away.

Lucy moved quickly as her sister, pale, perspiration beading her brow, collapsed. She pulled Maria close before she could hit the floor.

One of the officers that had entered the room reached for the emergency cord and pulled it. He hurried to their side. He was young and his worried gaze swept over her sister.

"Can I help?" he asked. "Miss, can you tell me your name?"

A weak smile hovered on Maria's lips. "Not on our first date."

The officer smiled at that and Lucy felt the air seep back into her lungs.

"I'm glad you can joke," Lucy told her sister.

"I'm okay." Maria closed her eyes as she said it.

"No, you aren't."

A nurse rushed into the room. Lucy was holding Maria and it didn't take the nurse long to assess the situation. She called for a wheelchair.

"We'll take care of you." The nurse smoothed Maria's hair. "How many weeks?"

"Twenty-one," Maria whispered. Her eyes darted to Lucy. "I'm scared, Luce."

"Don't be," the nurse assured her. "You're in the best place. We'll get you hooked up to a monitor and examined and I bet you'll be going home in a few hours."

"What are you going to do?" Lucy asked, because this was new territory for them both.

The nurse helped Maria into a wheelchair that an aide brought to them. "We're going to take her down to labor and delivery and make sure everything is okay. We'll monitor and make sure she isn't having contractions, check her blood pressure, and a few other things."

Maria nodded but her eyes were on Lucy, pleading for help. And Lucy didn't know how to help.

"I don't want to lose my baby," Maria said as the nurse pushed her toward the door. "Lucy, I want you to raise my baby. I've prayed about this. I really have. I'm not ready to be a mom."

"I'm not sure anyone is ever really ready to be a mom, Maria. That's why babies take nine months to get here." She'd heard that once. Maybe from Emma McKay, Daron's wife.

"No, it's more than that. I'm giving my baby up for adoption. But I want you to adopt her."

The nurse put a comforting hand on Maria's shoulder as they entered the elevator. "Honey, you have a few months to make this decision. For now let's just take a deep breath and remember the goal is to keep this baby healthy. Are you having a boy or a girl?"

"A girl," Maria whispered. "A little girl."

They didn't have nine months to prepare; they had four. Maybe less.

Lucy had never felt so alone.

When Dane arrived at the hospital to visit Elaine, he'd discovered that Elaine, her mother and Jerry were all being charged for arson. As he headed down the hall, he bumped into Alex Palermo.

"Alex, I didn't expect to see you here."

The younger man pushed the elevator button. "They've admitted Maria. She was having contractions this morning. I think Jerry upset her and it escalated from there. What are you doing here?"

"I wanted to visit Elaine, then found out she was arrested. I never saw that one coming."

"I'm not really surprised. There are still a few people around who are followers of the great Jesse Palermo." Alex pushed the button for the second floor. "I thought maybe you were here to see Lucy."

"I guess I am now. I want to at least check on Maria."

Alex shrugged, as if it didn't matter to him, but Dane thought Alex liked giving people that opinion of him. Just like Lucy wanted everyone to think she was the tough and detached soldier and bodyguard. Every now and then he thought the real Lucy appeared. She was compassionate, kind and loved her family. She loved the ranch and raising decent horses. She loved old farmers and simple women like Bea Maxwell. He knew those things about her, but she always denied that part of herself existed.

When they got to labor and delivery the nurse pointed him to a waiting room. Waiting was the last thing he wanted to do. But he sat down because this wasn't his fight. It wasn't his family. And yet he was here, waiting.

Alex stretched his legs out in front of him and put his hands behind his head. "Maria has been through a lot. She's been forgotten more often than not. I guess we're to blame for that. We all got busy doing our own thing and we expected our mom to be a mom. Some people don't know how to be parents."

"I think she'll be fine," Dane answered. "And you've all done your best."

"Right, our best. I'm not leaving after this. Maria needs someone who will stay put and be her family."

"Lucy is here."

"She won't stay. And I don't blame her. She's worked hard building her business. But I don't mind staying. I had a pretty good year and I put some money in the bank."

Dane didn't know what to say. About Lucy not staying, or about Alex having a good year. Instead he let the conversation drop. The television was on. The program was a court show with a dramatic judge. Mindless entertainment. Exactly what he needed.

"Can I ask your advice?" Alex said as they waited.

"You can ask. I'll try to answer."

Alex leaned forward. "I have a line on some good bucking bulls. I know that's going to make Lucy mad. But I have a knack for training them. I've been working with a friend and he's been teaching me."

"So what's the question?" Dane didn't see the problem.

"Well, it's going to make Lucy mad."

"I guess that's something you'll have to work out with your sister, isn't it?" It was Lucy speaking. She entered the room like a storm cloud, giving her brother a look that set him to squirming like a five-year-old caught putting gum in a girl's hair.

"Lucy, don't be mad. It's just…this is what I want to do."

"Right, of course it is." She put her hands up. "Don't explain. It isn't any of my business. It's your life. Your money."

"Lucy," Dane warned. She gave him a look that explained that in no uncertain terms it wasn't any of his business.

"How's Maria?" Alex asked.

Her expression softened. "She's going to be okay. So is the baby. She needs to rest and drink more water."

"Can I go see her?" Alex was already on his feet.

"Yes, hit the buzzer and tell the nurse who you are. They'll let you in."

Alex was braver than Dane would have guessed. He stopped in front of his sister and hugged her before leaving the room.

They stood staring at each other after he left. The door opened, a family entered the room, not seeming to notice them. They were loud, laughing and talking about the baby that was on its way. Dane took Lucy by the arm and led her from the room.

"Let's walk."

He steered her toward the vending machines. They could probably both use a cup of coffee, even if it was instant.

"He doesn't need bucking bulls," she said as she waited for coffee. "And I don't need to calm down."

"Long night?"

Her face started to crumble but she didn't cry. She squeezed the bridge of her nose, eyes closed, and when she was calm she faced him. "Yes, a long night. Maria. She wants me to adopt the baby."

"You would make a good mom."

"I don't know about that. The idea is frightening. What if I can't? And also, I have a business. Sometimes I travel."

He noticed she didn't mention Bluebonnet or the ranch. He was starting to connect the dots.

She was running scared, trying to escape the emotions.

"Let's start with the bucking bulls. It's his dream."

Her gaze darted at him and then away. "Yes, it's his dream. But it's dangerous. And expensive."

"Your brother isn't your dad. And you aren't your mom."

She sipped the instant coffee and didn't respond.

"Lucy, Alex isn't going to buy bulls and suddenly become a mean drunk. Let him pursue his dream. What can it hurt? And what would it hurt to let someone love you?"

She set the coffee down on the table and stared at him as if he'd just grown two heads. "You don't love me."

"I do, and I'm not sure what to do about it. You're trying to find the nearest escape route. That doesn't bode well for the future."

"I'm not good at this," she admitted. "I'm not good at relationships and I don't want to hurt you. Or Issy. I also don't want to be hurt."

"Right. But in the end, you're causing your own pain because you close all the doors before they can even open."

"I have to go." She tossed her coffee cup in the trash. "I told Maria I would be right back."

"There's the door." He pointed and she took his advice and left.

But he hadn't planned on her leaving. He had hoped she would see what was right in front of her, a man wanting to be a part of her life. Instead she saw monsters under the bed and couldn't let herself stop running from the past.

He understood, because he'd done his own hiding. His own running. Until Lucy, he hadn't ever imagined letting a woman into his life, into his daughter's life.

Now he couldn't imagine his life without her.

Chapter Seventeen

Lucy stood on the balcony of her apartment, coffee in hand. In the courtyard, people lounged around the pool and others sat in groups in the garden areas. Gas fires burned in the fire pits, even though it was a June evening and the temperature was in the eighties. She turned to go back inside, where Maria was lounging on the sofa, binge watching romantic comedies.

They'd been here for two weeks. Just Lucy and Maria. Lucy had brought Maria to her apartment because it was closer to the hospital and because she had to work. It was a good solution, since the doctor had put Maria on temporary bed rest that first week out of the hospital and asked that she come in immediately should she start having contractions.

Maria looked up from her show and patted the sofa. "You could sit down."

"I can't."

"Because you're worrying about work, the ranch, Alex, Marcus, me. What don't you worry about?"

Lucy shook her head and bit back a grin. Maria was pretty good at deciphering her moods. "I don't worry, I contemplate."

"You contemplate all of the things you have to worry about."

"I guess. But right now I have to contemplate a job I have in Dallas. Will you go with me, stay here or go home to Bluebonnet?"

"Home, I guess, since I'm not having any problems. Not that I don't love city life, but I'm a country girl at heart and I miss my dog. And Issy." She gave Lucy a meaningful look but Lucy didn't bite.

"I can take you back tomorrow."

Maria sat up. "Will you stay in Bluebonnet or come back here?"

"Probably come back here. After the Dallas job."

Maria drew her knees up, a sign that she was settling in for a long conversation. Lucy headed for the office and her paperwork.

"I need to get some plans drawn up for a job," she called out, hoping Maria would let it go.

"What's the job?" Maria had followed her to the office. She sat down in the chair next to the desk, again curling up.

"A corporate guy. Big business. People hate him."

"Nice." Maria studied the papers on the desk. "Is he young and single? Handsome?"

"No, he isn't. This is real life, not a fairy tale."

But for some reason Maria's words made her think of Dane. Because she missed him. She had missed a few people in her life. Usually family. Sometimes a friend. She'd never missed anyone with this empty ache that wouldn't go away.

"Oh, you do miss him." Maria chuckled as she made the observation.

"What?" Lucy slid the plans to the side of her desk. "Stop. I need to work."

"No, you need to confront what's right in front of you."

"A younger sister who won't go away?"

Maria picked up a pencil and tapped it on the desk as she studied Lucy. "No, confront your feelings. You love Dane Scott. I think you've always loved him. You doodled his name in your notebook when you were sixteen."

"I did not." She got up from the desk. She tried to escape but there was nowhere to go.

"You did. I read your journal." Maria's expression fell and her eyes narrowed. "I'm sorry for reading it, and I'm sorry for everything that happened. I'm not sorry that it ended when I was little so I didn't have to live through it."

Lucy sat on the edge of her desk. "You lived through our mother, her relationships and her flighty behavior."

"I always had Essie, though. She's been more of a mom to me than anyone. And you've been a mom for the last couple of months. You don't realize this, but you're good at it."

Speechless, Lucy stared at her sister, trying to find the right words.

"Maria, thank you."

"You're welcome. And that isn't a plan for a security job. Remember, I read your journal a dozen years ago. I'm still snoopy and you do occasionally leave me alone. You're coming up with a plan to help the women at the shelter. Empowerment classes. Self-defense. Self-motivation. I like it."

Lucy rubbed her hands down her face and shook her head. "That's it. We're going back to the ranch."

"Right now? You're taking me home?"

"Get your clothes. I can't take it anymore." Lucy

walked out of the room. Stormed actually. It felt good. It felt empowering. And it felt as if she'd just shocked her little sister.

Lucy woke up in her bed at the ranch. She woke up to the dog snuffling around in her room, a rooster crowing in the distance and someone singing from the kitchen. It wasn't the radio because it was pretty close to horrible. She forced herself out of bed and down the hall.

"Stop!" she growled at her brother.

Alex looked up from the pan of eggs he was frying. "Hey, when did you get here?"

"Last night. Stop singing or I'm going to hurt you."

"I'm thinking that if you don't want me to raise bucking bulls, I might go to Nashville and record an album. Justin McBride did it."

"Justin can sing."

"No, really, listen." He started singing again.

It might have been a George Strait song but if it was, she didn't recognize it. Lucy made a face but he just laughed and kept singing.

"Stop."

"I have another one you might like better." He started in again.

The dog ran down the hallway barking. From the back of the house Maria asked if there was a cat dying. Lucy gave him a meaningful look but he kept singing.

"I think bucking bulls are a great idea," she shouted, and gave him a playful shove. "So stop. Don't ever sing again. Not here, not in the car, not at church. Never. Sing. Again."

He broke into a church song. Lucy stepped back.

"What is that?" she asked. Because it was completely different. It was good.

"My real voice." He grinned. "Gotcha."

"I'm surrounded by siblings intent on driving me crazy."

"Did you ever think we're trying to drive you *sane*?"

"I'm sane. It was confirmed by two different therapists. Slightly broken but not beyond repair." She poured herself a cup of coffee and took his plate of eggs.

"She's going to start an empowerment class for the women at the shelter," Maria said as she came down the hall.

"I should have left you in Austin." Lucy walked off with her eggs and coffee.

Alex and Maria joined her at the table. Alex shoveled food in his mouth as if it were his last meal. When he finished he carried the plate to the sink, poured coffee in a thermal mug and slipped his feet in boots he'd left by the back door.

"Where are you going?"

"To get my bulls," he said. "I paid for them a month ago. I thought I'd let you think it was your idea so maybe you wouldn't be all cranky. But cranky seems to be your favorite emotion."

"I'm not cranky."

"Oh, but you are. You choose it."

She didn't know what to say.

"Don't try to argue your way out of this, sis. You use cranky as a defense mechanism. Skunks spray, turtles duck into their shells, you get cranky. It makes people leave you alone. And I'm not saying it doesn't work for you, but it seems like you might want to dial it down a notch."

"Thanks," she mumbled, then she got up and did what he hadn't expected. She hugged him. "For real. I'm working on this, but it helps, knowing you've got my back. And you're not afraid to pound me over the head."

Alex winked. "Someone has to do it."

"I guess they do." She looked at her watch. "I need to call Boone and let him know I won't make it for a meeting today. They'll have to call me on video chat. If you all need me, I'll be at the church talking to Pastor Matthews."

"You're serious about these classes?" Alex asked as he headed for the door. He was walking backward and walked into a wall before she could warn him.

"Yes, I'm serious about the classes." She also had her own stuff she needed to deal with. If she was going to talk to broken, battered women about empowerment, she needed some empowering from within.

She pulled up to the church an hour later. Pastor Matthews met her at the door to the fellowship hall. His wife was with him. She had coffee ready and she'd even brought doughnuts. "In case you haven't had breakfast," she said.

"I have, but thank you." Lucy sat down at the table across from them.

For the next hour she poured out her story and she cried as she'd never cried before. Because she needed healing from the past. She needed to be an example, humbling herself and finding her own strength. She needed to believe in herself.

"Do you know what I think, Lucy?" Pastor Matthews spoke quietly. "I think you've gone through a lot, but you've always been stronger than you give yourself credit for. Everything in life has led you to this moment, to finding who you want to be and where you want to be. I think that's a conversation you need to have with

God. I also think this idea you've had is a great idea. I think when we opened the door to abused women, we didn't think about the deeper issues. We were just thinking they needed a safe place. You've helped with the security and self-defense but I can see how these women need more. They have to believe in their own value."

Lucy sat back with her cup of coffee. For the first time in a long time, something felt perfectly right. It was about more than a job, or an obligation. This was a door to help women who had been in abusive situations. She hadn't come home expecting this, but maybe God had brought her home to show her this path.

Dane pulled up to the Palermo Ranch. Lucy was home. He hadn't known until he saw her truck next to the stable. He considered leaving, but he'd never been a chicken and he wasn't going to start being one now. Instead he parked next to her truck and got out. He was here to see Alex's new bulls. Lucy lived here. He couldn't avoid her.

He didn't want to avoid her.

He found them both in the corral behind the stable. The bulls, three of them, were grazing the meager supply of grass in the small enclosure. Alex was on the tractor moving a bale of hay. As he approached the corral, Lucy turned his way, her eyes widening when she saw him.

Standing there looking at her like that, he couldn't really make sense of what had happened between them. The only thing he could think of was that he wanted to kiss her. A breeze picked up and blew her hair, then she pushed it back with one of those hands he loved so much. Strong but gentle.

If he had to describe her to anyone, that would be it.

And when she looked at him with wariness in her dark eyes, he felt gut stomped. Flattened.

He didn't know what to say to her.

"You're back" were the words that slipped out.

"Yes. I brought Maria home. She was getting on my nerves." A hint of amusement twinkled in her eyes, replacing the wary look of moments ago.

"I can't imagine," he said. "I came to see how the bulls are settling in."

"Like bulls. They want food and water." Her hand still held her hair as she glanced back to the bulls, the tractor. "Issy's pony seems to be missing her."

"Does he?"

She nodded. "You should bring her by. I miss her, too."

"I'd like for us to talk, Lucy."

Her nod was barely perceptible but it was an agreement so he took it as such.

"Tomorrow," he continued.

"Pushy."

For the first time in weeks he felt a hint of hope. "Yes, very. I need to talk to you before the real estate agent and the buyers come to my house."

"You have buyers?"

"Yes. I have buyers."

Alex joined them. He looked at each of them and shook his head.

"Well, sis, what do you think?" Alex leaned against the corral, careful to avoid the electric fence strung around the top.

"They're bulls. And I think you'll do great with them."

"Thanks." He knocked his shoulder against hers. "How'd it go with Pastor Matthews."

She shot him a warning look, but it was too late. Dane waited to see what she would say. When she didn't, Alex offered up the information.

"She's going to start lessons for the women at the shelter. She thinks they need more than self-defense. Empowerment. Right, Luce. It wasn't a secret, was it?" He hit his hand to his heart. "My bad. I mean, everyone is going to know. Stuff like that gets out in a small town like Bluebonnet."

A noise came out of her mouth that sounded a bit like a growl. "No, it isn't a secret. But it is my business and not yours."

"I think that's a great idea. Not that it matters what I think," Dane chimed in.

She cocked her head to one side and studied him. Alex took the hint and walked away.

"It matters." She said it softly, simply. "It matters to me what you think."

He stroked a hand down her cheek. "Can we talk? Not right now. We both need time. But we left a lot of things unsaid."

"Plenty was said."

"Yes, but more needs to be said."

"We can talk," she agreed. "We do need to talk."

He wanted to kiss her. But he didn't. He said goodbye and walked away.

Chapter Eighteen

"Do you want to go to town for lunch?" Lucy asked Maria the next day. They had watered the garden, although it didn't look like much more than a weed patch. Alex was working with his bulls. A neighbor was helping him. The boy had graduated a year ahead of Maria.

It seemed to Lucy that Maria had spent more time watching the neighbor than watering the garden. "That sounds good. I think Aunt Essie has open-faced roast beef sandwiches on the menu today." Maria was already slipping on her shoes.

"Let's go before she runs out."

They jumped into the truck and drove to town. "Did you know that Dane is looking at a school in Dallas for Issy. Because there isn't much around here for her."

"I did know."

Maria rolled down the window and leaned her head back. "Lucy, I'm still praying you'll decide to take the baby."

Her sister was like a dog with a bone on that topic.

"I'm praying about it, too," she said as she pulled into a parking space in front of the feed store. Silence descended in the truck.

"Really?"

"Yes, really." She got out before Maria could pull her into a hug and make it awkward.

Some people were bothered by PDA, public displays of affection. Lucy was more bothered by RDA. Random Displays of Affection. She was working on that.

"Lucy! Hey, Lucy!" Bea Maxwell hurried down the sidewalk, a big grin on her round face. Her hairnet hung to one side. She wore two different socks.

"Bea, it's good to see you."

Bea hugged her, not caring that Lucy disliked it. And then she turned on Maria and pulled her close for a long hug.

"Maria, Essie says you're having a baby." Bea hugged her tight. "I hope you get to keep it. I didn't get to keep my baby. My mama said she just couldn't raise us both."

Maria looked wide-eyed at Lucy, who shrugged. She gave her attention back to Bea, who didn't seem fazed by the information. It must have been quite some time back. Bea had to be close to sixty.

"Apparently—" Bea slipped back to her favorite word "—I wasn't an easy baby. My mama said all the time she could barely keep track of me. Maria, I hope you were an easy baby and that you have an easy baby."

"Thank you, Bea." Maria hugged the older woman. "Do you want to walk with us to the café?"

"I should do that. Essie doesn't like when I'm late. I set an alarm to keep me on track because timeliness is next to godliness."

Bea kept on with the questions. "Are you staying in Bluebonnet, Lucy? You've been gone a long time. Some folks said you ran away in the night. I tried that once but my mama dragged me home."

Lucy smiled. "I joined the Army, Bea."

"Did you really? Do you shoot a gun?"

"Yes, I do."

"Will you stay and take care of Maria and the baby?" Bea couldn't be sidetracked.

"Yes, Bea, but don't tell anyone."

They walked through the doors of the restaurant and Bea nearly came apart at the seams. "Hey, you all, did you know that Lucy Palermo is staying in Bluebonnet to raise Maria and her baby?"

Maria groaned and buried her face in her hands. Lucy ignored the curious stares and just smiled. But her gaze connected with a pair of curious blue eyes. Dane sat at a table with Chet Andrews and Pastor Matthews.

Well, wasn't that just wonderful.

Essie rounded up her cook and gave Lucy a parting look that said they would talk later. Lucy waved her aunt off and headed for the coffeepot. She picked it up to fill her cup and Chet called out to her.

"Hey, Lucy, if you're going to be around awhile, could you fill a guy's coffee cup."

Lucy filled his cup. "Why not, Chet. I live to serve. Anyone else?"

Pastor Matthews lifted his half-empty cup. "Well, since you ask. And would you mind getting me a piece of that apple pie?"

"Apple pie, coming up." She cast her eyes at Dane but moved on.

"Hey, what about me?" he asked, reaching for her hand.

His touch nearly undid her. "I guess you can have pie."

"I meant, what about me?" He winked at her, and Chet laughed.

"I'm not sure what that means, but I'll get you a piece

of pie and some coffee." She escaped, breathless and a little bit giddy.

When she returned to the table Dane was paying. "Never mind that pie. I have to go."

Was he mad? She couldn't tell from the look on his face. She looked from him to Chet and then to Pastor Matthews. They shrugged and went back to eating pie and gossiping. Why did men always accuse women of talking too much?

She ran after Dane, ignoring the curious looks of people in the café. She'd spent her entire life avoiding stares, trying to be invisible. Today she didn't care.

As Dane went out the door she caught up with him and followed him down the sidewalk.

"Where do you think you're going?" she asked, reaching for his arm.

He hesitated and looked back at her. "I have a meeting today, remember?"

"Yes, with me."

He glanced at his watch. "And the real estate agent. Lucy, I have to go."

"Fine. Then go."

She stood on the sidewalk watching him leave. She waited until his truck pulled out from the parking lot before going back inside.

"What was that all about?" Essie asked when she returned.

"I don't know."

Her aunt gave her a questioning look. "You're a mess, Lucy Palermo."

"I know, but I'm working on it."

Her aunt patted her shoulder. "Yes, you are. I think it is a real accomplishment that you kids are as whole as you are."

"Thanks, Aunt Essie." Lucy accepted the plate the waitress put in front of her. "And thank you for making the best open-faced roast beef sandwich in the state."

"Now you're just buttering me up." Essie hurried off to tend to customers.

Lucy took the salt shaker from Maria. This was their new normal. And she found she liked it. She loved the relationships she was building with her family and even her community.

What she didn't like was not knowing where she stood with Dane.

Dane pulled up to the Palermo ranch. In the backseat, Issy asked if they were there yet.

"We're here." Dane got out and unbuckled his daughter. They were there, but they weren't expected.

"Does Lucy know I got cowboy boots?"

"No, she doesn't know. But you can tell her when we get inside."

He set her down and she reached for his hand.

"I won't get them muddy?"

"No, you won't. It hasn't rained." He led her up the steps to the front door. As he raised his hand to knock, the door opened.

"Dane." Maria just about glared at him.

"I have new boots," Issy said, breaking the ice by holding up a foot. "See? Are they flower colors?"

Maria lost her hard edge as she knelt to look at the purple boots.

"They are most definitely flower colors."

"I'm going to have Cobalt. Lucy told Daddy."

"Did she really? That's pretty amazing. Do you want to walk out and see the pony so we don't have to be stuck in here with the grown-ups?"

Issy leaned close to Maria. "Yes, because Daddy has a secret."

"Does he?" Maria stood and eyed him speculatively.

"Issy, you aren't supposed to tell."

Issy bit down on her lip. "I didn't tell the secret. I said you had one."

"That is true," Maria told him. "Come on, Issy, we'll go see Cobalt. Dane, you have fifteen minutes. Make the most of it."

"Thanks, Maria. I knew I could count on you."

He watched the two of them walk across the lawn, and then he walked through the open front door. He heard pots and pans clanging in the kitchen and someone singing to the radio. At the door he stopped and watched as Lucy put away dishes and sang. When she turned and spotted him, she jumped.

"I come in peace," he said with his hands up.

"You could have announced yourself."

"I like watching you."

"Spying, you mean."

He shrugged.

"What are you doing here? Where's Issy?"

"She's with Maria. They went to see Cobalt."

"That didn't really answer my first question." She tossed the dish towel on the counter and waited.

He was there because it felt right. Because nothing else would be right until he talked to her.

"I love you," he said, without preamble. "But you already know that."

"You've mentioned it before."

"You're going to be difficult, aren't you?"

She smiled, finally. "I'm always difficult and you're making me nervous."

"Good, that makes two of us. Nervous, that is."

"Oh no." She started backing away. "No."

"I thought I'd at least ask you a question before you started objecting."

She shook her head.

He reached for her. Strangely, she didn't object. He pulled her into his arms and kissed her. She kissed him back.

And that kiss didn't feel like a no.

"I've missed you," Lucy whispered as he lifted his head for a brief moment, right before he kissed her again.

"I've missed you, too. I've missed us. Our friendship, the laughter, everything about you. Even your objections. But I have a plan to conquer your objections."

"Do you?" She wondered what his plan was, because if it had to do with his kisses, being held by him, she might not object.

"I do," he said.

"I need to tell you something first."

"Let's go outside." He led her out the back door. The sun was going down and the air had cooled off.

He didn't let go of her hand. As if she'd try to get away from him.

"What did you need to tell me?" he asked as they walked along the fencerow.

"Maria asked me to adopt her baby."

"I knew that."

"I said yes."

He gave her hand a squeeze. "I'm glad. That wasn't an easy decision for her. Or you."

"No, it wasn't."

He pulled her close to his side and led her to a tree near the edge of the lawn.

"There's more."

"Okay." He leaned against the tree and drew her to his side, wrapping his arm around her so that she was held close.

In the distance they heard laughter. She looked across the lawn to the barn where Alex was leading Issy on the pony.

"I love this life," she said. "I love my job, too. I don't want to give up, either." She turned in his arms and put a hand on his cheek. "I also don't want to give you up. I'm the worst kind of selfish. I want it all."

"I want you to have it all."

His words settled in her heart like a promise.

"What about the buyers for your ranch?"

"I turned them down and told my agent to tear up the contract. I'm not selling." He leaned, touching his forehead to hers. "I want you to have everything you've ever wanted. I don't want you to give up something you have worked hard for. I don't want you to give up your ranch and your family. I want to help you have it all."

His words tore a sob loose from deep inside. She didn't cry because it wasn't a moment for tears. But no one had ever given her a gift greater than his words, his support, his understanding.

"I'm tearing down your objections, Lucy. One by one I'm tearing them down. Because you can be whoever you want to be, as long as we're together and we have faith."

Together. The word stunned her. She'd never seen herself living in this place, with a man at her side, someone she could depend on.

She'd had Boone and Daron but they were more like brothers. They had their own lives, their own families.

Dane wanted to be the man that she leaned on.

And she wanted him to lean on her.

She stared up at him, at the reflection of what she felt for him shining in his blue eyes.

"I'm afraid to be a mom." She admitted her biggest fear.

"You are already a mom at heart. You're a mom to Issy, to your brothers and sister."

"I might sometimes have to go out of town."

He kissed her again. "We'll go with you. And we might also have to stay in Austin because that's where the best school is for Issy. But we have Alex here to help with the ranch. I have good people who work for me. There's nothing we can't overcome."

"You might not realize this but you've been tearing down my walls without even trying." She leaned against his shoulder. "I love you, Dane."

"I love you, too. You can be a bodyguard. But I'm going to be your protector. I want you in my life and in Issy's life. I don't take that lightly, Lucy."

"I know you don't. And when I say that I want to be in your life, I mean it more than anything I've ever meant in my entire life."

"I love you, Lucy Palermo, and I want you to marry me."

"Yes." She looked into his eyes as she said it. "I'll marry you."

Epilogue

Lucy stood at the back of the church, Daron McKay at her side. She'd stood in this vestibule many times in her life but she'd never expected to stand there in a wedding dress. She'd never expected this kind of happiness or the man at the front of the church to be waiting there for her.

Standing at her side was the prettiest flower girl ever. Issy with her spiral blond curls, a basket of flowers hooked over one arm. Issy had taken to calling her Lulu and that was just fine. As long as no one else tried to call her that. She'd had to warn everyone, especially Boone Wilder, that she was Lulu to no one but Issy.

"Are you actually in a dress and not packing?" Daron teased as they waited for the bridesmaids to walk down the aisle ahead of them.

"I'm not packing. If I was, you'd be in trouble."

He chuckled softly and patted her hand on his arm. "You make a beautiful bride and I'm really happy for you, Lucy. Dane's a good guy and I know he'll treat you right."

"Of course he will. I'm trained in hand-to-hand combat."

"And there's the part where he loves you."

She smiled softly at that. "Yes, he does."

Her bridesmaids had started the march down the aisle to the front of the church. Daron's and Boone's wives and Maria wore dresses in autumn red. Lucy looked to the front of the church, where Dane waited. He saw her and his smile grew, making her want to run down the aisle to him.

"Don't rush the gate," Daron said. He held her hand on his arm and kept her next to him until the bridesmaids were in place and the wedding march started.

Out of spite, Daron forced her to make the walk at a sedate pace. When they reached the front of the church, he kissed her cheek and handed her off to Dane.

The ceremony began and Lucy couldn't stop looking at the man who was going to be her husband. She lost herself in the blue of his eyes, in his smile, in the way it felt to have his hands holding hers.

"Repeat after me." Pastor Matthews paused, smiled at Lucy and said, "Lucy, are you sure this is what you want to do?"

She glared at him, and he laughed. "Of course it's what she wants," he said.

Pastor Matthews recited the vows for Lucy to repeat. Holding Dane's hand, she managed to say them as a few tears trickled down her cheeks and conspicuous moisture gathered in Dane's eyes.

She said, "I do," and Dane's eyes widened. That was the reaction she expected. But he was no longer looking deep into her eyes with love and devotion.

Lucy turned to see what had his attention.

Maria stood between the other bridesmaids, her eyes wide. "My water just broke," she whispered.

"Oh no, you don't. Pastor Matthews, quick, finish

this ceremony. I'm not letting her get away." Dane took her by the shoulders so that she faced him and not the situation about to change all of their lives.

"Dane, do you take this woman to be your lawfully wedded wife, to have and to hold, sickness and in health, poverty and whatever, until death do you part?"

"I do." Dane grabbed his wife. "I do."

"I now pronounce you man and wife. Kiss the bride and go have a baby."

Dane kissed Lucy, a much longer kiss than she thought was necessary under the circumstances.

"I'm afraid we're going to have to skip the reception," Dane told the people gathered for the wedding. "You all have cake. Enjoy the food. We'll see you in a day or two."

He kissed her again, then they gathered up Maria and headed for the waiting limousine that had been rented to take them for a few nights in Austin.

Six hours later Maria kissed her little girl on the head and handed her to Lucy. The baby had dark hair and dark eyes. She was wrinkled, red and possibly the most beautiful baby Lucy had ever laid eyes on.

"Maria, are you sure?" Lucy swiped at the tears trickling down her cheeks and leaned to kiss her sobbing little sister.

"I'm sure." Maria held tight to the hand of Jaxon Williams, the baby's father, because he'd asked to be with her when she had the baby. "We're sure. We want you to raise her. I'll be her aunt Maria. Jaxon has to go soon. He's being deployed."

Maria swiped again at the tears. "I'm really okay. I just know I can't do this."

Dane hugged her, filling Lucy with more love than

she could have imagined. "Maria, you did what you felt was best and it was a difficult thing to do."

Maria's gaze lingered on the baby. A tiny little girl named Jewel. A nurse had taken her and gently placed her in a tiny crib that she pushed toward the door.

Lucy gave her sister another hug but Maria pulled back.

"Go and hold her close, Lucy. I need a few minutes and Jaxon is here."

Lucy hesitated to leave her sister but Dane nodded, indicating they should give Maria space. The nurse had already moved ahead of them, pushing the baby and her bed from the room. They were taken to a room down the hall where they would spend the evening. Haven and Alex were there with Issy, who couldn't wait to see her little sister.

Lucy settled into a chair with baby Jewel as the family surrounded them.

Life was good.

* * * * *

*If you loved this story,
pick up these other books
from bestselling author Brenda Minton:*

*HER RANCHER BODYGUARD
THE RANCHER'S FIRST LOVE
THE RANCHER'S SECOND CHANCE
THE RANCHER TAKES A BRIDE
A RANCHER FOR CHRISTMAS*

*Available now from Love Inspired!
Find more great reads at www.LoveInspired.com*

Dear Reader,

Lucy Palermo is a character I couldn't leave behind. She's someone we might want to have as a friend, but we know that she wouldn't give that friendship easily.

There are people in our lives who are very much like Lucy. They appear strong, distant, or cool. If we take the time to get to know them we will find that they hide their pain beneath that cool facade.

Every day we pass people on the street, see them in the grocery store, ignore them in the hallways at school and we think we know them. We judge what we see on the outside. The popular girl in school must have it all. The boy walking by himself in worn jeans and a stained T-shirt, we pass on by without a greeting. The woman at the store who never smiles when we say hello, she must be unfriendly.

They all have stories. And often, they just need a friend. Today, take time and be the person who reaches out.

Brenda Minton

COMING NEXT MONTH FROM
Love Inspired®

Available August 22, 2017

SECOND CHANCE AMISH BRIDE
Brides of Lost Creek • by Marta Perry

Widower Caleb King is set on raising his two small children without assistance from anyone—especially a relative of the wife who'd abandoned them. When Caleb is injured, Jessie Miller is just as determined to help her late cousin's family—never imagining that coming into their lives would lead to her own happily-ever-after.

THE TEXAS RANCHER'S NEW FAMILY
Blue Thorn Ranch • by Allie Pleiter

Wanting a better life for his daughter, horse trainer Cooper Pine moves to the small Texas town of Martins Gap. But he doesn't count on his daughter becoming a matchmaker! Once little Sophie decides she wants neighbor Tess Buckton as her new mommy, it isn't long before Cooper starts to see Tess as his future wife.

HIS SECRET ALASKAN HEIRESS
Alaskan Grooms • by Belle Calhoune

When private investigator Noah Catalano is hired to spy on waitress Sophie Miller, he has no idea he's about to fall for his assignment—or that Sophie is actually an heiress. Will the possibility of a future together shatter when their secrets are exposed?

HER HILL COUNTRY COWBOY • by Myra Johnson

In taking the housekeeper job at a guest ranch, all former social worker Christina Hunter wants is a quiet place to recover from her car accident. What she gets is a too-attractive single-dad cowboy, his two adorable children and a chance at the life she's always dreamed of.

THE BACHELOR'S UNEXPECTED FAMILY
by Lisa Carter

Suddenly guardian to his teenage niece, crop duster Canyon Collier is thankful to have single mom Kristina Montgomery living next door. The former Coast Guard pilot never expected that while bonding over their teens and giving the beautiful widow flying lessons, he'd begin to envision them as a family.

HEALING HIS WIDOWED HEART • by Annie Hemby

Doctor Lexie Campbell planned to spend a quiet summer volunteering at a free health clinic—until forest fires force her to move. Her days become anything but calm living next door to hunky firefighter Mason Benfield—to whom she's soon losing her heart.

LOOK FOR THESE AND OTHER LOVE INSPIRED BOOKS WHEREVER BOOKS ARE SOLD, INCLUDING MOST BOOKSTORES, SUPERMARKETS, DISCOUNT STORES AND DRUGSTORES.

LICNM0817

Get 2 Free Books,
<u>Plus</u> 2 Free Gifts—
just for trying the Reader Service!

Love Inspired®

YES! Please send me 2 FREE Love Inspired® Romance novels and my 2 FREE mystery gifts (gifts are worth about $10 retail). After receiving them, if I don't wish to receive any more books, I can return the shipping statement marked "cancel." If I don't cancel, I will receive 6 brand-new novels every month and be billed just $5.24 for the regular-print edition or $5.74 each for the larger-print edition in the U.S., or $5.74 each for the regular-print edition or $6.24 each for the larger-print edition in Canada. That's a saving of at least 13% off the cover price. It's quite a bargain! Shipping and handling is just 50¢ per book in the U.S. and 75¢ per book in Canada.* I understand that accepting the 2 free books and gifts places me under no obligation to buy anything. I can always return a shipment and cancel at any time. The free books and gifts are mine to keep no matter what I decide.

Please check one:
- ☐ Love Inspired Romance Regular-Print
  (105/305 IDN GLWW)
- ☐ Love Inspired Romance Larger-Print
  (122/322 IDN GLWW)

Name _____ (PLEASE PRINT)

Address _____ Apt. #

City _____ State/Province _____ Zip/Postal Code

Signature (if under 18, a parent or guardian must sign)

Mail to the **Reader Service:**
IN U.S.A.: P.O. Box 1341, Buffalo, NY 14240-8531
IN CANADA: P.O. Box 603, Fort Erie, Ontario L2A 5X3

Want to try two free books from another line?
Call 1-800-873-8635 today or visit www.ReaderService.com.

*Terms and prices subject to change without notice. Prices do not include applicable taxes. Sales tax applicable in N.Y. Canadian residents will be charged applicable taxes. Offer not valid in Quebec. This offer is limited to one order per household. Books received may not be as shown. Not valid for current subscribers to Love Inspired Romance books. All orders subject to approval. Credit or debit balances in a customer's account(s) may be offset by any other outstanding balance owed by or to the customer. Please allow 4 to 6 weeks for delivery. Offer available while quantities last.

Your Privacy—The Reader Service is committed to protecting your privacy. Our Privacy Policy is available online at www.ReaderService.com or upon request from the Reader Service.

We make a portion of our mailing list available to reputable third parties that offer products we believe may interest you. If you prefer that we not exchange your name with third parties, or if you wish to clarify or modify your communication preferences, please visit us at www.ReaderService.com/consumerschoice or write to us at Reader Service Preference Service, P.O. Box 9062, Buffalo, NY 14240-9062. Include your complete name and address.

EXCLUSIVE LIMITED TIME OFFER AT
www.HARLEQUIN.com

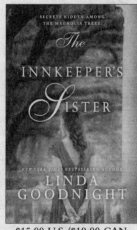

SECRETS HIDDEN AMONG
THE MAGNOLIA TREES.

The
INNKEEPER'S
Sister

NEW YORK TIMES BESTSELLING AUTHOR
LINDA
GOODNIGHT

$15.99 U.S./$19.99 CAN.

$1.⁵⁰ OFF

New York Times Bestselling Author
LINDA
GOODNIGHT

welcomes you to Honey Ridge,
Tennessee, where long-buried secrets
lead to some startling realizations in

The INNKEEPER'S
Sister

Available July 25, 2017
Get your copy today!

Receive **$1.50 OFF** the purchase price of
THE INNKEEPER'S SISTER by Linda Goodnight
when you use the coupon code below on Harlequin.com

SISTERS17

Offer valid from July 25, 2017, until August 31, 2017, on www.Harlequin.com.

Valid in the U.S.A. and Canada only. To redeem this offer, please add the print
or ebook version of THE INNKEEPER'S SISTER by Linda Goodnight to your
shopping cart and then enter the coupon code at checkout.

DISCLAIMER: Offer valid on the print or ebook version of THE INNKEEPER'S
SISTER by Linda Goodnight from July 25, 2017, at 12:01 a.m. ET until
August 31, 2017, 11:59 p.m. ET at www.Harlequin.com only. The Customer will
receive $1.50 OFF the list price of THE INNKEEPER'S SISTER by Linda Goodnight
in print or ebook on www.Harlequin.com with the **SISTERS17** coupon code.
Sales tax applied where applicable. Quantities are limited. Valid in the U.S.A. and
Canada only. All orders subject to approval.

® and ™ are trademarks owned and used by the trademark owner and/or its licensee.
© 2017 Harlequin Enterprises Limited

HQN™

www.HQNBooks.com

PHCOUPLGLI0817